Crossroads

David Brelsford

Crossroads

& other stories

All royalties from the sale of this book will be donated to the Motor Neurone Disease Association of Tasmania.

See page 106 for information about motor neurone disease.

Crossroads & other stories
ISBN 978 1 76041 177 0
Copyright © text David Brelsford 2016
Cover photo: West Australia Desert endless road © Andrea Izzotti

First published 2016 by
GINNINDERRA PRESS
PO Box 3461 Port Adelaide 5015
www.ginninderrapress.com.au

Contents

A Different Drummer

The wild wind whistled through the long row of pine trees, and he stopped, gasping. The wind made waves of sound in the branches, under the stars.

He dropped to his knees on the bare earth, listening intensely, concentrating. An untamed sound, primitive music, now swelling, now dying, rising, falling, sweet, pure and free. His hands felt for the soil and he clutched it desperately, lovingly.

The wind rose, the music reached a crescendo; and as he knelt, the soil in his fingers and his face toward the stars, a tear trickled from his eye.

He knew there was not much time.

They were almost here now. He could hear them. But no longer did he try to run. Instead he knelt, digging his fingers into the soil, looking at the stars and listening to the untamed free music of the trees. And crying. Crying.

They came and stood over him, menacingly, and with obvious satisfaction. But there was the trace of fear on both of their faces. Fear of the unknown.

'It's all over, Reynard,' said the older man. 'Come on, we don't want to be out in this place all night.'

Reynard did not move.

The wind rose into the trees again and the two policemen shuddered.

The younger one put a hand on his shoulder. 'Come on, Reynard,' he said. 'We don't want to use force, but…'

Reynard twisted and looked up at them. He could still feel the soil in his fingers. 'If a man does not keep pace with his companions, perhaps it is because he hears a different drummer,' he said straight to their faces.

The older man stiffened. 'That's treason!' he gasped, unbelieving. 'You'll get twenty years for that alone.'

But Reynard only smiled to himself as he rose and went with them. He was beaten. He'd had his run. Now he must pay the price.

The older man shivered: not from cold, but from apprehension. 'What a desolate place this is!' he said. 'Must be a kilometre to the nearest apartments!'

The younger one looked at him in surprise. 'That far?' he said, and then he shuddered too. He turned to the captive. 'What makes you go to such places as this?' he asked. 'What's the attraction of this – this wilderness?'

But the older man was impatient. He strode faster. 'Don't worry about asking him questions,' he said. 'Let's just get back, quick.'

They walked in silence for a few minutes, and then suddenly the captive, Reynard, said, 'I love the sound of the trees and the feel of the wind in my face.'

The older man ignored him. Mad, he thought. Insane, no doubt about it.

But the younger one had had no experience with madmen. He tried to reason with him. 'But that's silly,' he said. 'No one goes to places like this.'

'Our ancestors did,' said Reynard defiantly.

Now the older man joined in. It was fun to bait a madman sometimes. 'But that doesn't give you any more right to do it than it does to chop off your wife's head just because George VIII used to.'

'Henry,' said his companion.

'Huh?'

'It was Henry VIII who chopped off his wives' heads.'

'Oh,' said the older man. 'Well, who was George VIII then?'

'He was the last of the British kings before they did away with monarchy altogether.'

'Oh,' grumbled the older man. 'I was never any good at ancient history anyway.' Then he turned his anger on the captive. 'You!' he spat. 'Why can't you live like everyone else! Why do you have to come out to a desert like this! Do you realise it's nearly a kilometre to the nearest apartments? This must be the most deserted place on earth!'

The prisoner was silent.

It made the older man angrier. 'I bet you don't even know your number, do you?' he shouted. 'You're a bum! You'll be telling me next you know music!'

But Reynard was quiet. As they walked, he glanced furtively at the stars now and then, and running through his brain was a Beethoven symphony. Beethoven's Ninth. 'All men shall be brothers.' He was the lowest of the low, and he knew it. Now that they had captured him, he would have to pay.

A Letter to Joseph

Jerusalem
Saturday

Dear Joseph,

Greetings to you from Rueben, son of Jotham. If you remember, I worked with you about five years ago. That was when your boy Jesus was with you, of course.

I hope my mention of your Jesus does not upset you, because it is about him that I want to write. No doubt you have heard of the stir he caused this past week in Jerusalem; and by the time you get this letter you will have heard of his death last night.

I know you must be frantic with worry about your good wife Mary. Allow me to put your mind at rest: she is here safe in Jerusalem, although grief-stricken over the death of her boy. She was there when he died last night – I saw her. He was very concerned about his mother, Joseph. He asked one of the bystanders – I think he probably knew him – to treat her as though she was his own mother. I saw them together later – much later, after they had taken away your boy – consoling each other in their grief. So please don't worry, Joseph, the young man is taking good care of her and I am sure she will be back with you in a few days.

Up to yesterday I had only seen your Jesus once since I left Nazareth five years ago. That was the time – maybe you heard of it – when we were all terribly hungry but did not go away because we did not want to miss what he was saying. Those bodyguards he had with him all the time were getting worried because they had hardly any food, and even after they came round and collected what we had so they could share it out, they only had a few scraps. I heard the crowd saying there was only enough for two or three men, and a bit of panic was starting to creep in, but he just told his gang to split it up and share it out and we all had a good meal. I do not know how he managed it. I heard someone near me say it was a miracle, but I do not know: I was too busy eating the bread and fish to worry about whether it was a miracle or not. But I know that what he said that day made a tremendous impression on me and made me think very deeply. He affected most people like that. I cannot remember any exact words he said but I know it seemed so right at the time. I got the impression that whatever you asked him he would have a good answer for.

I never saw him again until yesterday. I had been working on a couple of new houses up north a bit – I am still working as a carpenter – and I intended to come to Jerusalem for the whole of the passover week, but a clumsy labourer dropped a piece of wood on my foot and I had to lie up until the swelling went down. It meant that I did not get into Jerusalem until Friday.

When I got there, there was only one topic of conversation in the whole city – and that was your son. Apparently he had been stirring up a real hornet's nest, upsetting the wrong people, and they reckoned they were going to crucify him that afternoon. I could not get to see him before they took him to that hill outside Jerusalem – Calvary, they call it – because my foot was very sore again after the journey I had made into town. But I did manage to get there just as he arrived. They had been spitting on him – I got quite close and saw somebody hit him full in the face with a gob of spittle – and they were milling round and taunting him and jeering at him. There was blood on his head and I thought maybe they had been beating him but when I looked again I saw that they had jammed some sharp thorns over his head and were calling it a crown. A crown of thorns. They had been whipping him too, and he was weak and I could see that he was suffering.

How my heart wept when I saw my old workmate in such a predicament! I remember the times when we had worked together, when he could have out-hammered, out-sawn and out-lifted you and me put together. It is funny: not many people seemed to appreciate his physical strength; they seemed to think he was weak and puny. But they say that earlier in the week he had gone into the temple and overturned the money-changers' tables, and you know how heavy those things are!

Anyway, they got to the top of the hill and then they laid the cross down and nailed him to it. I saw a crucifixion once before and it took about eight of them to hold the poor wretch down and nail him on, but Jesus did not struggle at all. He seemed resigned to it. But when the blood spurted from his hands, he gave a terrible shudder and I thought I was going to be sick. I was not watching when the soldiers lifted the cross up to stick it in the ground when he would first take the weight on his hands. I had to turn away.

Joseph, I do not ask for much out of life, but I do hope that I do not die by crucifixion. The authorities ought to have it stopped.

I am not going to try to describe the next few hours. I was so shocked I am not sure my brain registered it properly. But I do remember him telling this young man to look after his mother. And I seem to remember him praying – actually praying! – for God to forgive them! What a man! I know if I were up there, forgiveness would have been the last thought on my mind!

They had stuck up a notice above him which said, 'This is Jesus the King of the Jews.' My old workmate a king?

They were jeering at him and laughing but he didn't seem to mind. He still retained that sort of spiritual confidence that you and I used to remark on even before he left you. That was the outstanding impression I got of the whole thing – the way he took it, so bravely and calmly, as if he knew all along that this was how it would end.

I did not dare to say that I knew him because they are hounding all of his old mates. That gang who was always with him deserted him completely. I heard that one of them killed himself, but the city is seething with rumours and you do not know what to believe.

I think I will stay here a few days and then come up to see you. Hope you are giving the younger fellows some of the harder jobs now. If you take care, you will still be good for a few years yet.

I have almost finished, but I want to say that he was a tremendous man, Joseph, a tremendous man. It seems such a waste for him to have gone like that. Still, he may have made a lasting impression on a few people.

Your old friend,
Rueben

Back From the Brink

Catmouth is a pleasant little town, bordered on one side by the River Catt and the other side by the big chicken farm that gives employment to half the town. I've lived here for about eight years, since dropping out of university. You get used to it. I work at a steady little job; it doesn't pay much, but it keeps me alive. And I have my cats.

The cats kept me going through the dark days when I first came here. I was still hurting after leaving uni. In fact, I suppose I still do. But time does heal, gradually.

The cats were something that would love me, but more importantly something that I could love. I needed that. I inherited them from the previous tenant of the house and they've been with me ever since. But cats grow old, and a couple of weeks ago Toby, the male, died.

It shook me. It made me look at Millie the female as though for the first time. Suddenly, instead of just an object of comfort, she was a living, breathing animal. And she too was getting old.

'Not much longer to go, Millie, old girl' I said to her.

And I realised I could be almost saying that to myself. Then I told myself not to be ridiculous. 'You're thirty,' I said to myself.

And another voice said quietly, 'And still single.'

But I needed two cats. And poor old Millie needed a companion. So I looked in the paper and went to a run-down, ramshackle house on the edge of town and rescued a male kitten that was being given away.

Millie didn't take to him kindly at first, spitting and growling. But I consulted her about what to call the newcomer. Monty came to mind.

'We'll call him Monty, shall we, Millie?' I said.

Then I pulled up short. Surely you've not got to the stage where you're talking to your cats, I thought. That's for old women. You're only thirty.

But poor Monty was not a happy cat. Millie was desperately jealous of him, of his youth and energy. I figured they'd settle down. And they did, but not in the way I had wanted.

I rose one morning and for the first time found Monty asleep cuddled up to Millie. At first I was elated. But when Monty refused to stir, just lying there and looking up at me, I became worried. He was obviously sick. And though I smiled at the way Millie had suddenly taken to mothering him, I knew I had to get help.

Now ours is a small town. There is no vet. But there is a very decent little library. So I headed downtown and logged on to their catalogue and brought up feline sicknesses. The library had three books which I determined to get, but somehow I sensed there was something wrong. I looked at the catalogue again, and I saw what the problem was.

I guess that was the moment in my life when I came the closest to being a fussy old maid. Because I went to the counter and demanded to see their cataloguer. The library was quiet and I waited to berate her. But it wasn't a her at all. It was a man who came to see me and ask what the problem was.

'There are mistakes in your cataloguing,' I said. I tried not to sound too stern.

He smiled. 'How do you know?'

'I studied librarianship at university,' I said. 'I know the cataloguing rules. Look here. You've put round brackets where there should be square brackets. And here: you've put only three dots, like this…when there should be four.'

He looked closely at the screen. 'Ah,' he said. 'You're right. I'll rectify that. Thank you, Mrs…'

'Miss!' I emphasised. 'Carol Pringle.'

'Well, thank you, Carol,' he said. 'It would have been a catastrophe if I'd done that in my exam.' He looked at me. 'I only just passed, you know.' Then he took a deep breath. 'My name's Jeremy Darbyshire. My friends call me Jerry.'

'Right, Mister Darbyshire,' I said. 'I'll get those books now.'

But they did no good. Monty continued to waste away. I couldn't afford to go to the expensive vet in the big city. I pored over the books but failed to find a remedy. It became painful to watch Monty. His breathing became laboured. Millie, his adopted mother, guarded him carefully, licking him and staying with him all the time. But it was obvious he was dying.

'Poor Monty,' I said. 'And Millie, you have been so wonderful to him.' And suddenly I realised I was crying. And equally suddenly, I realised it was the first time I had really cried since those so painful days when I had dropped out of uni.

Monty died.

I went to work and continued my routine life as in a dream. But I was grieving. Toby had been an old cat and common sense told me he would have died soon. And Millie was old. But Monty had been young and full of life. It was a catastrophe. I had needed him so that I could give him love. And now that outlet for love had been taken away.

I determined not to get another cat. Not straight away, at least.

Then I got a reminder in the mail that the books from the library were overdue.

Now I'm a great believer in energy attracting energy. Some people might call it karma. Or fate. But anyway, I was walking to the library early this frosty morning intending to drop in the books before I started work.

And I heard a voice call my name. It was the cataloguer. He walked rapidly up to me. 'I fixed those mistakes,' he grinned.

'Well, it wasn't a real catastrophe,' I said. 'Only a cataloguer would notice or think it was important.'

'How come you don't work in a library if you studied it at university?' he asked.

I suddenly found my heart beating a little faster. 'I dropped out before qualifying,' I said.

'Ah!' he said, and then was silent.

He seemed to sense that I didn't want to say anything more about that. I didn't want to explain why I had dropped out of uni. Or why I had come to this quiet little town to lick my wounds and try to heal.

We were at the entrance to the library. He seemed to be gathering himself up for an important question. 'Would you meet me for lunch?' he asked. Then he grinned and almost laughed. 'We could discuss cataloguing!'

And I found myself saying yes! Amazing!

And I thought about him as I went about my work. I know that male chauvinism is still alive and well, especially in small country towns. Many a man would have resented being told by an unqualified female that he hadn't done his job properly. But he had taken it in good spirit. And he wasn't bad. Mid-thirties, and single (I found myself hoping).

And I wondered if he spelt his name with an 'e' , as in the English county, or with an 'a', as it is pronounced. Such things are important to library cataloguers, even unqualified ones.

And perhaps I'll tell him the real reason why I dropped out of university, I thought. About Colin, whom I had loved with my heart, my soul and with every fibre of my being, and who had let me down so badly that I'd just had to get away. Perhaps I'll end up telling Jerry about that.

Time does heal. Even broken hearts.

And perhaps his cataloguing mistakes, and perhaps Monty's death, would turn out not to be such catastrophes after all.

*

Postscript: Well, did it work out? I'll give you a clue. I know how to spell his name now!

Crossroads

John Adamson was already an old man by the time he came to Crossroads.

It was John who called it Crossroads, because two roads running north–south and east–west intersected there, and because no one else lived nearby to give it a name.

Mr Adamson had been a university lecturer in his day, teaching literature and poetry. But now he was retired and had decided to come to the quiet country to live out his final years.

Mr Adamson – let us call him John – had been a good man and a good lecturer. He often used to say that he was pointing his students towards a better life by introducing them to the great writers, poets and philosophers of the world. If the students wanted to take notice of what the greats had to say, that was fine. And if not, well, that was their decision. It had been John's job to let them know that such riches existed and to give educated observations on how best to use them.

But now John was retired. And he had come to Crossroads, a lonely place with nothing outstanding about it. It wasn't unpleasant, but even so it made you think that perhaps he could have done better in his choice of location for his retirement.

After he had settled down, John realised that one very important part of the local set-up was missing. There was no signpost at the crossroads to tell which way went where. John himself wasn't sure where the roads east and west went to or came from, but he knew that the road north led to a small town called Valhalla, and that the road south led to a place called Salem.

Being a public-spirited man, John decided to agitate for a signpost. But the local council wasn't interested. 'It's such a lonely place out there. Nobody goes there. And besides, we don't have the money.'

John Adamson was not put off. He decided to make and install a signpost himself. He got the wood, painted the pole white, and made the sign with black printing against a yellow background. He painted, very carefully, the signs to Valhalla and Salem; and because he didn't know what else to put, he just put East and West for the other directions.

Then he took his spade, the ingredients for a concrete base, and the sign itself, and went down to the crossroads. He dug the hole, mixed up the sand, gravel, cement and water, and poured it into the hole. Then he got his sign and set it carefully into the wet mix, making sure it pointed the right way, and bracing it so that it stayed stable while the concrete set.

While he was doing all this, someone was watching him. It was an old woman, a hag almost. Her name was Naomi and she lived in a hovel about a mile away. She had lived in the area all her life, and those who knew her said she was mad. She sat behind a bush watching John Adamson working.

'What's the fool doing?' she wondered. But she was very quiet, and because they knew she would never harm them, the birds and little animals chirruped and scuttled around and John was never alerted to the fact that there was someone else nearby.

John was proud of his work and decided to stay by it until the concrete set, just to make sure everything would be all right. The whole project had taken him six hours, from first cutting the wood to finally setting the sign in place. He rested for an hour and then ate some food he had brought, spitting out the seeds of the apple he was eating. And still Naomi silently watched him.

Evening came on and John tested the concrete. It was virtually solid now. So John took away the bracing, stood back to admire his finished job and started walking home. He felt very pleased with himself. 'I have lived a good life,' he thought. 'I pointed my students towards the gods of poetry and high intellect. And now I have pointed the way to Valhalla and Salem for the wayfarer. It is up to them what to do with that information.'

Then he went home and hanged himself.

Meanwhile, Naomi sat quietly. Because she was mad she didn't mind staying there all night. And she stayed all through the next day, sitting quietly, looking at the signpost, wondering if the man would come back. But of course he never did. So on the morning of the third day Naomi, the mad old woman, went to the signpost and sawed it down and took it home for firewood. 'This wood will keep me warm for three days,' she said to herself. 'And a sign isn't necessary there. Everybody knows the way to Valhalla or Salem.'

Now the story might have finished there but for a very unusual incident that happened at that spot a few years later. One of Mr Adamson's brightest students happened to be in the area, travelling from west to east, when he came upon the crossroads. It was late in the evening and Aaron was very tired. He decided to camp at the crossroads and he fell into an exhausted sleep as soon as he had pitched his tent.

When he awoke the next morning, he stood up and stretched and suddenly thought he saw a woman watching him from behind a bush. He moved there and saw old Naomi retreating.

'Hello,' he called. 'I'm very hungry. Do you have any food?'

Naomi stopped. She didn't say a word but just pointed to an apple tree bearing ripe fruit. Then she was gone and Aaron never saw her again. He had no way of knowing, of course, that the apple tree had grown from one of the seeds that John Adamson had spat out all those years before, and that this was the first year it had fruited.

He ate an apple and looked around with revitalised eyes. This was a blessed spot, he thought. You could raise crops here. The apple tree was proof of that. And being a crossroads there would be travellers coming through who would buy your produce. Aaron decided to stay and make it his home.

In time, other travellers came and some of them stayed, encouraged by Aaron's enthusiasm and growing prosperity. Soon it became a thriving village. Aaron got married, started a family and was elected mayor of the community.

And still Naomi, who didn't seem to have aged at all, lived in her remote hovel and occasionally went to see what was happening at

Crossroads. 'What are the fools doing now?' she would ask herself as she sat unobserved watching all the activity.

As mayor of Crossroads, Aaron had some successes and some failures. He wanted to change the name of the place to Adamson, in honour of his old professor who was the original settler. But the locals voted against it. 'It's always been called Crossroads,' they said. 'It's traditional.' So Crossroads it stayed.

Aaron had heard of the sad fate of the original sign, how vandals had stolen it within days of it being erected, and he decided against replacing it. Instead he built an information centre. 'People won't be able to knock that down and take it away,' he said.

He decided to name it the John Adamson Memorial Information Centre. Aaron had loved his old professor as only a good student can love a good teacher. So the information centre was built at the crossroads itself, and on the spot where the signpost had been was a big blue sign that said 'The John Adamson Memorial Information Centre', and an arrow pointing towards the rather grand building that claimed to give the passing traveller every piece of information they needed – including how to get to Valhalla or Salem.

After Aaron's term as mayor was ended, he announced that he was moving up the road to Valhalla to further his career. The local people were very sad to see him go. Aaron attempted to comfort them. 'My work is done here,' he said. 'And Valhalla's not all that far. You can contact me if you want any advice. I'll come back from time to time to see you. And keep that information centre going: it's the best thing I ever did.'

But three days after he had gone, mad old Naomi came in the middle of the night and sawed down the sign that said 'The John Adamson Memorial Information Centre' and took it home as firewood. 'This wood will keep me warm for a week,' she said to herself. 'And a sign isn't necessary there. Everybody can see where the information centre is.'

Empty Threats

About ten months ago, we acquired a springer spaniel puppy. She was cute, cuddly and totally adorable. And as cute, cuddly and totally adorable puppies will do, she has grown into a gangling, hyperactive and totally recalcitrant adolescent.

For some reason known only to a doggy mind, she has taken a fancy to my little crop of silver beet.

I found her chewing one again the other day, and I roared, 'If I catch you doing that again, I'll skin you alive, twice.'

She dropped her ears, put her tail between her legs and adopted the openly guilty look that only a really attractive springer spaniel can do.

But it set me thinking about my (empty) threat. Surely it's impossible to skin someone alive, twice. Once would be more than enough. But I know where I got the expression from. It harks back to my schooldays, when it was the favourite expression of our geography teacher, Mr Butler.

Old Buttle, as we called him (not to his face) was a tartar. If you as much as blinked three times inside five seconds instead of the designated two, he was onto you. 'If you do that again,' he would roar, 'I'll skin you alive, twice.'

I had lost small bits of skin now and again and I knew how painful it was, so the idea of being skinned alive terrified me. And to have it done twice! It didn't bear thinking about.

I didn't learn much about geography in Mr Butler's lessons, but I sure as hell learnt how to sit still and be quiet (and to only blink twice inside each five-second time frame).

Then Merryweather joined us. He was a new boy just moved into the area from the bush, and he was innocent of the ways of Old Buttle. Moreover, he was a bit of an arguer. The type of guy who, if you told him that zebras were striped black and white, would immediately argue that they were striped green and yellow. But he wasn't stupid. You could tell from the glint in his eye that he was just having you on, just arguing for the sake of arguing and having a giggle to himself behind his hand.

I liked him.

But it was inevitable that Merry and Old Buttle wouldn't get on. To put it mildly.

It didn't take long. In only the second lesson, Merry did something wrong. He probably blinked three times in quick succession or something like that, and Mr Butler pounced.

'If you do that again, boy,' he said through gritted teeth, 'I'll skin you alive, twice.'

Merry said something that only someone of his innocence and intelligence could say. He said, 'Aye?'

'If you do that again,' Mr Butler repeated with frightening emphasis, 'I will personally skin you alive, twice!'

Then Merry did something that none of us had ever dared to do in five years under Old Buttle. He smirked. He smirked! In fact, he almost sniggered.

Merry was fresh from the bush, remember, and would have been used to skinning rabbits and wombats, goats and probably horses. He knew what was involved. And so he smirked.

Mr Butler didn't like that. His teeth grew pointed, flames shot out of his ears and he rather vociferously invited Merry into his office.

It was right at the end of the last lesson on a Friday afternoon, so we hightailed it for home and left Merry to his grisly fate. As schoolboys will.

It was Sunday afternoon at the local cricket match when I saw Merry again. He looked quite normal. Maybe being skinned alive twice wasn't as bad as I had thought.

'How'd it go on Friday?' I asked.

'What do you mean?'

'With Old Buttle,' I said. 'Did he skin you alive?'

Merry laughed. 'Nah. It's all empty threats. He just asked me to try not to do it again, and sent me home.'

The bastard! Mr Butler, I mean. All these years he'd terrified us poor little schoolboys with the threat of this horrible punishment, and all the time he'd never meant it!

Well, I knew better now. No more sitting rigidly to attention in Old Buttle's classes. I actually relaxed a bit. And I actually learnt a bit of geography for once. I can still remember some of it. The capital of Mongolia is Ulan Bator, in case you need to know. Another thing you don't have to bother looking up on the internet.

Anyway, to get back to our lovely young springer spaniel. She's just full of youthful energy, that's all. But I caught her eating the silver beet again yesterday. 'If you do that again,' I shouted at her, 'I'll skin you alive, twice!'

And she dropped her ears, put her tail between her legs, and slunk away. She didn't know it was an empty threat.

'It's all in the tone of voice,' said my wife, Josephine. 'It's not the actual words.'

I thought, 'Bullshit,' but what I actually said was, 'I'm not so sure about that.' She's my wife, remember.

'Try it sometime,' she said. 'Next time you catch her, tell her that you'll do something nice, but say it in a threatening tone. See what she does.'

I had to wait a while. It was nearly twenty minutes before the dog started chewing the silver beet again. And I was right onto her. 'If I catch you doing that again,' I roared in my best threatening voice, 'I'll give you a saucer of cream and a big juicy T-bone steak!'

And, lo and behold, she dropped her ears and slunk away with as guilty a look as ever.

Well, it's not very often my wife is wrong, but she was right this time and I had to admit it.

It applies to humans too, of course. Most people don't listen to what is said to them. Wives, try it. Say to your husband something like 'I murdered the children, twice, this morning before school, and then again when they came home. It was a horrible gooey mess.' And he'll probably look up and say, 'That's nice, dear.'

On reflection, maybe in some families it would be a nice idea.

Josephine tried it on me. There I was, sitting reading the paper and she said, 'If you don't help me to wash the dishes, I'm going to make your favourite meal, iron your best shirt and then take you to the bedroom for a night of unrivalled sexual mayhem such as you've never experienced before. At least, not with me.'

And I fell right into the trap. I said, 'Sorry, dear, I'll try not to do it again.'

She sat down opposite me. 'You didn't hear a word I said, did you?'

''Course I did,' I said.

'What were they?'

I was ready for that one. 'Look,' I said, 'I've got more important things to worry about than that. Do you think Hawthorn will beat Collingwood this weekend?'

But she wasn't being put off that easily. Besides, she doesn't know a thing about football. 'Come on,' she said. 'What did I say?'

My mind went into fast rewind. 'You said you were going to make my favourite meal and iron my best shirt, but I knew you were kidding because we haven't got the things here for my favourite meal, and my best shirt doesn't need ironing. So I knew they were empty threats.'

I'd got her there. I figured all she could do was admit defeat.

But she had one last card to play. 'What about the other threat?'

I searched my mind. 'Something to do with sex, wasn't it?'

'Yes,' she said.

'Was that an empty threat too?' I asked slightly breathlessly.

'Well…'

At this point my story has been heavily censored.

From Within

First Day

It wasn't my fault when I killed that jogger. Sure, I'd had a few drinks and I was driving over the speed limit. But everyone drives over the speed limit, don't they? And what were the joggers doing on the road anyway? Roads are for cars. Couldn't they run in the bush or somewhere? Fitness fanatics, that's all they are.

And it wasn't my fault. I only took my eyes off the road for a split second, didn't I! And there they were. How was I supposed to avoid them?

But the judge was having none of it. He wouldn't listen. They never do. Judges and rich bastards have it in for guys like me. I tell you, I've heard more tales of victimisation by those bastards than you would believe.

Ten years, the judge gave me. Out in seven if I'm a good boy. Whoop-de-fucking-do. I'll be nearly thirty by then. My life will be over. And it wasn't even my fault. If those joggers had been running on the other side of the road, I wouldn't have hit them.

Well, one thing's for sure. I'm not sticking around here for ten bloody years. But I'm not going to escape, if that's what you're thinking. That's a mug's game. No. I'm going to be a good little boy, aren't I? Oh, I know how to say yes sir, no sir, three bags full sir. And I know when to volunteer and when to keep quiet. I learnt that in reform school. It pisses me off of course. But in the long run it'll be worth it to get out in seven.

I saw plenty of guys come into reform school and look the screws straight in the eye and behave 'like a man'. And they got the shit kicked out of them. And no remission. I'm not stupid. I'll work the system and be out in seven.

But it still shits me that I'm here at all. A few drinks too many, two seconds of inattention, and my life is ruined. And not even a thank you from the judge for stopping instead of hitting the gas and getting out of there. That's gratitude for you. You can't do a thing right in their eyes.

And all the joggers could do was cry and carry on about what a great bloke he'd been. The guy I killed, I mean. It's a wonder he didn't have angels' wings on before he died, to listen to them. And his family all dressed in black and erecting a little roadside cross where it had happened. And them with at least two other kids. Not a glance in my direction and my ruined car and my ruined life. No family; no father, no brothers or sisters, and a mother who'd just as soon kick me in the teeth as visit me in here. Not even a fucking girlfriend. And my car, the only thing I had in life, confiscated and rusting away in some police yard.

I tell you, my life is ruined.

Four Weeks Later

Well, you would never believe it in a million years. I had a visitor. A fucking visitor! The stupidest woman I've ever come across. The dead bloke's sister, of all people. She came to say she's forgiven me. What an idiot!

I told her not to gloat and to fuck off. The screw heard me and gave me a hard look. I just hope he doesn't report me.

She left and she was crying, but what did the silly bitch expect?

Mind you, I'll admit she wasn't a bad-looker. Nice figure and well dressed. Perhaps a couple of years older than me. But what's that got to do with anything? She came to gloat and I told her to piss off. One up to me.

I hope she doesn't come back.

After Five Weeks

Well, I have never seen such stupidity in all my life. The stupid bitch came back!

This time I wasn't so blunt because the same screw was watching me. So I just sat down and said, 'Look, I don't like you coming here and gloating over my bad luck. Please go away and don't come back.'

That fixed her.

I couldn't see if she cried or not, but she went away without any fuss and I was glad to get back to my cell.

The Next Day

I'm not in trouble but I'm close to it! The screw came to see me and told me that if I sent her away again like that he'd report me for insolence. And that would be half my remission gone in one go.

So now I've got to be polite to this stupid girl.

The screw said she was trying her best and that I should wake up to myself. His name is Middleton. He's not bad, I guess, for a screw. A lot of them would have just dobbed me in the first time and never thought twice about it.

Five Days Later

I'm going to bed early tonight because it's visiting day tomorrow. A lot of the guys do that.

I wonder if she'll come.

I've been practising in my mind all week what to say to her, now that I've got to be polite to her. Because Middleton will be there watching me.

In a way, I hope she doesn't come. But I hope she does.

I don't even know her name.

One Day Later

Kathy. That's her name. At least we established that. And I was polite, but I couldn't think what to say.

She asked me how I was coping in here, and I said, 'Okay,' but then couldn't think of anything else.

So I asked her what she did for a living. She works in an office.

We were awkward. But when she leaned forward and wanted to talk about the accident, I just stopped her, politely, and said, 'Can we discuss that another time?'

And you know what she said? She said, 'So you want me to come again?'

I just nodded.

And then she smiled! It's the first time I've seen her smile.

And now that I think of it, it's been a long long time since I made any girl smile like that.

When we were all going back to our cells, Middleton just looked at me and nodded. I figure that means he approved.

Now I've got a week to think of all the things to say to her next time.

Next Week

Well, I had something to say to Kathy but it wasn't good news.

Gus Atkins has been released. Gus was a good bloke. He got the choir going and I was seriously thinking of joining them. I'm a good singer. And it would be something to talk to Kathy about.

And now he's left. And they're all saying that the choir is going to fall apart without Gus to lead it.

Shit!

Kathy looked genuinely sorry for me. She says she's not musical herself although her sister plays the flute in a small orchestra.

I asked her what she did in her spare time and she said she was studying to be a podiatrist. It's something to do with feet. Sounds boring to me. But I didn't say that. I've got to keep my nose clean, haven't I?

But we had a nice chat and I was sorry when our time was up.

Six Weeks Later

I really look forward to Kathy's visits now. We talk about everyday stuff but it's just nice to talk to a girl, and not swearing all the time or getting abused or getting ordered around. Just normal everyday conversation. It's so rare in here. So that's why Friday nights are always an early night for me, and Saturday mornings are the highlight of my week.

She's a really nice girl. I could have gone for her if I was on the outside. Although if I was, she probably wouldn't look twice at me.

At least she's still coming even though I killed her brother.

So she's got a big heart. And for a little while in the week I'm happy.

Middleton's okay too. He's seen that I'm making an effort, and although he's not spoken directly to me, he gives me the occasional nod. Coming from a screw that's a big compliment.

Three Months Later

I'm bored out of my brain. Every day is the fucking same. Except for Saturday, of course. And even that's fallen into a bit of a rut. We talk about regular things but it seems to be all the same somehow. If I was on the outside, I could suggest things and we could do things and our friendship could move forward. But not under these circumstances.

But she's an intelligent girl, because when it was time for her to leave she said, 'Give yourself a goal.'

How can I give myself a goal in a place like this? It's soul-destroying.

At least I'll have something to talk to her about next week.

One Week Later

I was a bit nasty to Kathy this morning and I regretted it straight away. I snarled at her. 'How can I give myself a bloody goal in here?' I said.

She didn't reply immediately. We talked about other things but I could see her mind was far away.

Then when she was leaving she said, 'Why don't you try to go the week without swearing?'

It was the worst departure we've had since those first few days. And it's shaken me. She's never said before that she didn't like my swearing.

How can I go for a fucking week without fucking swearing in this fucking place?

Well, maybe I can think it but I don't have to say it. I'll give it a go. I've got nothing else to do, have I.

Three Days Later

I've failed. I went for two days without swearing. Then when Riley, the bastard, started niggling me I couldn't help it. I told him to fuck off and stop deliberately stepping on my heels. This was at exercise. He just laughed and if I'd been outside I would have jobbed him.

But I'm still keeping my nose clean, and anyway Middleton was watching, so I ignored him and moved away. I guess that was a good move on my part.

But the little bastard made me swear. I'll have to tell Kathy that I failed.

Maybe I'll try again. If I can go for two days, maybe I can do better next week after I've seen Kathy.

Four Days Later

I don't know what to make of Kathy. I thought she'd be pleased that at least I'd gone two days without swearing. But she didn't seem impressed at all. She said, 'What about the rest of the week?'

Well, what was the point? Once I'd failed, what was the point until I started again this week?

And she said, 'Life doesn't run in neat weeks.'

Well, it does in here.

I was annoyed and resentful. But she softened a bit and said, 'Try again. And tell me how you go.'

Of course I'll tell her how I go. And I guess it is a goal to aim for. So I'll try. I did it for two days last time. I'll keep out of Riley's way. And just hope that nothing else happens.

Five Days Later

Well, I failed again but I can't help laughing about it. In fact, I'm almost pleased about it in a strange kind of way. Because things have happened.

Dave Crocker, my cell mate, was released. I didn't even know he was due. He was a quiet old bird, no trouble, and I didn't know much about him.

My new cell mate, a guy called Ray Fromarsh, already had permission to play some music. So he put this CD on of this singing. And it was great! I've never heard anything like it before!

When it was finished I said, 'That was fucking fantastic!'

Then I realised what I'd done. But I didn't care so much because the music had been so good.

Ray said it was something called Beethoven's Ninth. I've heard of Beethoven. But Beethoven's Ninth? His ninth what?

So Ray and I sat down and we talked a lot about music. I told him about Gus Atkins starting the choir but that it had folded when Gus was released.

Ray said he loves music but can't sing or play an instrument himself. I thought he might have wanted to start the choir again. But his only musical talent is in listening. And he's only here for two months. Which is a pity, because I'm learning a lot from him already.

Well, it's something to tell Kathy and at least I went four days before being overwhelmed by Beethoven. Which is a lot better than being annoyed by that idiot Riley. So I suppose I'm improving.

One Day Later

I'm confused.

Middleton spoke to me today and just said, 'You're doing well on your swearing project.'

How did he know? He's been watching me, I know, but surely not that closely. And I'm not so stupid as to tell anyone what I'm trying to do. Because if I did that, everyone would be needling me, much worse than Riley, just to get me to swear. It wouldn't be hard.

So I've kept it to myself. And even if Middleton had noticed that I wasn't swearing, he didn't know that I'd made a conscious goal of it.

So how does he know? There's only one possible answer and I find it hard to believe. But the only answer is that Kathy has told him.

How did she do that? I'll have to ask her tomorrow.

And I can tell her about Beethoven's Ninth Symphony too.

Something to look forward to. And something to be a bit worried about.

Early night tonight.

The Next Day

I think I'm going to start making a list of the surprises I've had since coming in here. Starting with Kathy coming to visit me in the first place.

And I had thought that maybe, somehow, Kathy and me might get together…but I'd never thought it through. How could I have ever expected her to wait for seven years, at the least, for the man who killed her brother?

But what a surprise when I learnt this: that Kathy and Middleton have been seeing each other! I was gobsmacked. I thought Middleton was married. I know he's mentioned a little son. But apparently his wife died two years ago. And now him and Kathy are dating. When I think of it, I can see Kathy with him and his little boy. She's the motherly type.

And when I sit down and really think about it, I guess that's what she's been doing to me. Mothering me, I mean.

Well, my real mother was never any good. And so I'm grateful to Kathy for that.

Maybe it's time for a new era in my life.

I told Kathy about Ray, my new cell mate, and about Beethoven's Ninth, and she seemed really pleased.

And surprises seem to be in the air, because when she was leaving, she said, 'I've got a surprise for you next time.'

I wonder what she meant? I can't think what it would be. But I haven't got time to brood about it.

Ray played me another piece of music. It was called Mozart's Requiem. And it was great too.

So I said to him, 'Is there much of this sort of stuff?'

And he laughed. 'Mate,' he said, 'you haven't even scratched the surface.'

Fabulous! If there's more of that music around, I want to hear it!

But I can't help wondering what Kathy's surprise is going to be.

One Week Later

Not all surprises are nasty. Some are really delightful. And Kathy's was. You know what she did? She brought her sister along. The one who plays the flute in the orchestra.

She's younger than Kathy, a bit slimmer, and really nice. Her name is Natalie.

And we started talking about music straight away. She knows Beethoven's Ninth and Mozart's Requiem, and she told me to get Ray to play me some Welsh male voice choir music. So I'll do that.

One Week Later

I couldn't wait to see Natalie again on visiting day.

Kathy was all eyes for Middleton, although they can't talk much at those times, but all I was interested in was Natalie. We seem to be on the same wavelength straight away, talking about music. She's mentioned a lot of things that Ray talks about too. Beethoven and Mozart and a lot of others, and a pair called Gilbert and Sullivan who did a lot of funny shows, apparently.

We even talked about her brother. His name was Colin. Surname of Robertson.

And I said something to Natalie that I've never said to Kathy. I said, 'I'm sorry that I killed your brother.' She cried and smiled at the same time, and then just simply said, 'Thank you.'

I was too embarrassed to say anything else. But to say that to her on only her second visit, when I couldn't bring myself to say it to Kathy after months and months: well, that says that perhaps we're kindred spirits or something.

She's coming again next week and I'm looking forward to it already.

One Week Later

It's been a great week. The best week I've had since coming in here. Ray got some Welsh male voice choir music and I thought it was great! We talk about music all the time and I'm learning fast. And I love it! Ray is the best thing that has ever happened to me. He's opened up this whole new world for me.

So when I saw Natalie yesterday, she told me about her orchestra. She said they're practising a thing called The Messiah for Christmas. I'll ask Ray about that. She said there's some great singing in it.

I had an idea there and then. 'Do you think I ought to try and start the choir again?' I asked her.

And, funny, she didn't say anything. It was nearly time for her to go and perhaps she needed to think about it. But I would have liked an answer. I'll ask her again next week.

And I'll ask Ray if we can listen to The Messiah.

Six Days Later

I've hardly sworn for two weeks now. An occasional word has slipped out but I'm not uptight about it any more. I've just got out of the habit, I think. And I've got Kathy and Middleton to thank for that.

Ray got the music of The Messiah and, boy, is it heavy! But that Hallelujah Chorus is unbelievable!

I asked Ray yesterday whether he thought I ought to try and start up the choir again. And he had the same look on his face that Natalie had had.

'What do you think?' he said.

What sort of an answer is that? I'm worried. Why won't anyone give me a direct answer? I'm going to ask Natalie again tomorrow and see what she says.

The Next Day

Now I'm getting really frustrated. Because Natalie won't give me a direct answer either. She just sort of evaded the question. Well, I suppose I can't really blame her. She doesn't know what life is like in here so how can she give me advice like that? But I would have liked a hint one way or another anyway.

Kathy and Middleton are really lovey-dovey now. They have to be careful under the circumstances but you can see it in their eyes even when they have a casual word to each other, which is all they can do in here, of course.

But Natalie's the girl I like to see now. She knows music from a slightly different angle from Ray. He's just a listener and an analyser, but she is a performer and a worker at it.

Visiting hour goes so quick when I'm talking to her. With Kathy, I used to find it hard to find things to say, but with Natalie it seems as though I can't cram it all in inside one short hour.

But I know what I'm going to do next.

Tomorrow.

The Next Day

What I was going to do, and what I have done, is talk to Middleton about whether he thinks I ought to try and revive the choir. And even he was evasive, but I think he's shown me what to do.

He said, 'It's not up to me to advise. It's up to you to decide. It's got to come from within.'

And that's a phrase that Ray has used, particularly when he was talking about Beethoven and Mozart. That it came from within.

So I've made an appointment with the governor. I'm scared out of my wits, of course. And even if he gives me permission, I'm going to need help. But Middleton's there, and there's still a lot of guys who were in the choir before. They know what to do. They just need someone with enthusiasm to lead them. And Ray will be great too, with his theoretical knowledge.

Two Days Later

I saw the governor today. I was so nervous I could hardly say the words. The last time we spoke, he was overbearing and domineering. I suppose he has to be to new guys, to let them know who's the boss.

But after I managed to blurt out what I wanted, he seemed to show genuine interest. He wanted to know how much I knew about music, and I told him about Ray and Natalie.

And he said, 'You know that Fromarsh' – that's Ray – 'is due out in a couple of weeks. He's got a good behaviour remission.'

That's a disappointment. It's come round so quick.

But the governor said I could start the choir again, and Middleton has agreed to oversee things so that we don't fool around. We won't be doing that.

But I'm sad that Ray's going already. He's the best mate I ever had. I'm going to make him promise to keep sending me music. And to visit me too.

So. Now I have to get the choir organised again.

Three Weeks Later

I've been so busy I haven't had time to write in here very much.

Ray, the best mate I ever had, has been released. He promised he would visit me regularly and keep sending me music. And he has done.

So now I get three visitors every Saturday. Kathy, who's more interested in Middleton now, Natalie, and Ray. By the time visiting hour is over, my head's in a whirl.

So that's okay, but I wish Ray was still in here. I miss him. My new cell mate is okay but he's not interested in music and we don't have much in common.

I've got the choir going and a lot of the men who were in it before are coming again. Ray taught me the basics of conducting, so I'm doing that. It's crude, I figure, but the men know what to do most of the time. We've been going over the songs they used to do with Gus Atkins. But I want them to do something a bit heavier. So we're going to start practising some of those songs the Welsh choir sang.

I've got lots of ideas for us. I thought that if we practised hard enough, we could perhaps get permission to do a concert together with Natalie's orchestra. The men would love that. And it would be good for everyone.

I'll have to ask Natalie what she thinks. If she reckons it's possible, then I'll have to ask the governor, and if he says it's okay, then we'll really have to practise hard.

The Next Week

I should have known. When you think about it, it's only too predictable. Nobody has said anything but I've got eyes in my head.

Even so, after the initial shock I think I'm getting over it, the same as I got over my fantasies about Kathy.

And they do make a great pair. Ray and Natalie, I mean. They haven't said anything to me, but it's obvious the way they look at each other that they're in love already. Ah well, at least I can say that I brought them together.

And Natalie says she'll see her orchestra leaders about doing a concert with us. So that's good.

Nothing for me to do but forget about any fantasies about Natalie. It was stupid anyway. I've still got over six years to do.

And I've got lots of work to do with the choir to take my mind off it. We're going to need more tenors for a start. I'm a tenor and I sing along with them while I'm conducting, but it's not the best idea and sometimes I have to suddenly stop singing while I concentrate on conducting. It's hard but I'm enjoying it.

Two Weeks Later

You would never believe who walked into choir practice today and asked if he could join.

Riley!

I've had nothing to do with him since that first incident. But in he came. And he's got a nice voice. A good tenor. If he behaves, he'll be an asset to the choir. And I won't let him misbehave. The choir's the only thing I've got now, so he's not going to spoil it for me!

Oh, Kathy and Ray and Natalie still come to see me. And that's all very pleasant and I enjoy it. And it's nice to see Ray and Natalie so happy together.

But the choir's the thing.

Three Weeks Later

Riley's proving to be a real bonus for the choir. I've got him singing a couple of solos, he's so good, and he's not playing up at all. Of course, Middleton or one of the other screws is always there to keep an eye on things, but Riley's almost as enthusiastic about the choir as I am.

I figure it's just what he needed to turn himself around. He was just a fool before, but now he's found this talent he's come good. His first name is Gordon.

Two Months Later

It's been so long since I wrote in here, but I've been so busy with the choir that I just haven't had the time.

Some good and some bad things: Gordon Riley's really come along in leaps and bounds with his singing. He's got a lovely tenor voice and he's learnt his solo parts very well. I'm proud of him.

Natalie says her orchestra will be willing to combine with us to do a concert for the men, and if that goes well, we could even get permission to do one outside.

I really want to do that, because the piece I've got in mind for an outside concert will need an orchestra and lots – and I mean lots –-of hard work from all of us. But I want us to combine with Natalie's orchestra, and probably some outside singers too, and perform Mozart's Requiem.

A requiem mass. I figure I owe at least that much to Colin Robertson. That's the man I killed.

That will depend on the governor, so we're practising hard to make this first concert a success.

The orchestra came in the other night to liaise with us and get our acts together, so to speak. It was great to actually see Natalie play the flute.

And Ray came along too. It's lovely to see them together, even though I still have a few wistful pangs.

Middleton and Kathy have announced their engagement. Kathy has really taken to the mothering role with Middleton's little boy. So that's all good.

The bad thing, at least from a selfish point of view, is that shortly after the concert, Gordon Riley is due to be released. I'm going to miss him. He's been a great asset to the choir and he'll be hard to replace.

Five Weeks Later

It's our big concert in three days' time. Funny, I'm not really nervous. Because I know we'll do well. We've practised properly and we all know what to do. I just hope the guys in the audience appreciate it. But that's up to them.

And if we do well, then I'll approach the governor about the big project of doing Mozart's Requiem on the outside. He's a decent man once he sees you're making a genuine effort.

But the big thing is this: Gordon Riley's being released in about a week's time. And he came to see me last night. He talked about his singing and said how much it means to him now. And he apologised for needling me that day. I'd forgotten about that.

But then he said, 'I've got no other talents. So do you think I ought to take professional singing lessons when I get out?'

And I heard myself say the same thing that Middleton said to me so long ago. 'It's not for me to advise,' I said. 'It's for you to decide. It's got to come from within.'

Getting It Wrong

It was when Tanya lost her temper with Dan that we in our share house saw his true talent for exacerbating the situation, as you might say.

The day was middling fair with few clouds in the sky and God in his heaven when Dan stalked in and asked Tanya if she'd done his ironing yet, as he wanted to go out. Dan had obviously never heard of women's lib.

Over the next hour, Tanya put him right on that score, to put it mildly. Her message really was very simple. It was, 'I rather discourteously decline to do your ironing for you, and I would like to explain to you why I have made that decision.' But Tanya expanded on that.

I had the misfortune to be in the same room – it was the kitchen actually – when Tanya launched into her attack on Dan's philosophy of life. I cringed and moved towards the fridge as Tanya's tirade gained momentum. The back of the fridge seemed like a good place to be.

Dan just stood there with a faint smile on his face. But Tanya was only just getting started. We had the radio going at about a million decibels but I couldn't hear a note as Tanya shoved her face into Dan's and screamed her disapproval at him.

Well, screamed is a mild word. The walls shook, bits of paint started flaking from the ceiling. The lounge room window broke with a snap. The man-eating Rottweiler next door ran whimpering into his kennel, mothers called their children in from the street, buildings shook, I heard the distant sound of helicopters, 'pocka pocka pocka pocka', getting closer, the American president phoned the prime minister to see if he could help, hard-helmeted SAS troops took up positions outside the house.

Horns had sprouted from Tanya's head, her teeth had become pointed and her fingernails had grown an inch. And still she screamed on.

And still Dan, simple stupid Dan, stood there with that faint lopsided grin on his face.

I moved the fridge and edged behind it. My ears started bleeding, my head was pounding, I put a cushion over my head and still Tanya's voice started my brain melting.

Crowds gathered outside the house. The SAS set up barriers and warned everyone away. They looked worried. Nazi Germany, Falklands, Iraq, all those had been okay. But this, this was something else.

But even Tanya had to pause for breath sometime.

I glanced out and saw a little light come into Dan's eye, and I cringed back even further behind the fridge. 'Don't, Dan. Please don't,' I muttered under my breath.

But Dan did.

After about an hour, when Tanya's harangue had died down to a mere deafening scream, she took another breath – and Dan sprang.

'Jeez, you've got nice tits,' he said.

Help Me Get My Shirt Off

Yes, I can see you, you bastards, checking all the instruments and doing all the right things to make sure I keep on living. But it's going to do no good. I've made up my mind to die, and when a man decides to die nothing can stop him. Not even you, you bastards, with all your precision instruments and your drugs and your fancy medical training. I want to die now, because I know.

If only I could tell you. If only I could communicate with you in some way so that you'd know that I don't want to live: then perhaps you'd let me die. Perhaps you'd sort of 'forget' to switch on a machine at the right time. But then perhaps, with your training and your pompous ethics, you'd still try and keep me alive. You bastards.

I know now. I know the truth. And it's changed everything. You'll be surprised at how quickly I'll go downhill now. You'll say, 'He fought so hard and so well. But now it seems he's lost the will to live.' I can almost hear you. Oh yes, I can hear you sometimes, you know.

Oh, I did have the will to live all right. But that was before. I had everything to live for, didn't I? As soon as I recovered consciousness, it was the first question on my lips. Only I couldn't make my lips move. The only thing I could do was to blink. But that's enough to someone who is close to you. My brother understood. But he never let on to you because he's my brother, and you're only cold and clinical and professional. You bastards. Only I didn't call you bastards then. I loved you because I needed you.

My brother's lips moved as he repeated the sentence over and over for me. He understood. 'Your wife was killed but your son is going to live.' Eventually I worked it out from his lips. Then – once – I actually heard him saying it! '…your son is going to live.'

If my son was going to live, then I was going to live. I had to! He needed me!

You noticed an improvement in me immediately. I could see it on your faces. Occasionally my hearing came back, just for a few brief seconds at a time. My progress was encouraging. But you thought I'd never again be more than just a vegetable. How little you knew! How little you knew what the love for someone can do for you.

The pain was terrible. Sometimes my very nerves screamed out. But I would not – I could not – let it get on top of me. When it got really bad, I tried to think of what my boy and I would do in years to come. I'd probably be crippled and not able to move too fast, but still we had tremendous times ahead of us. Oh, how I loved my son! How I came to cherish those visions. He pulled me through many an agonising hour. And you, dear doctors, you helped. With all your drugs and your gauges, you attended to the physical side of it. But my son was doing the important work. He was the one who was really keeping me alive, was making me improve steadily.

But the pain! One of my favourite visions to take it away was of my boy and me in a dew-filled, early morning field, just playing with a ball. It was as uncomplicated as that, but oh, how I loved him! Just a boy and his father enjoying simple things and being good friends: good mates, one to whom you could always tell your troubles. Many's the time you have wiped away a tear and thought it was a tear of pain, when in actual fact it was a tear of sheer love for my son.

He kept me alive.

But the pain! Oh the pain! With all your drugs and your instruments, you couldn't always stop it. I had to rely more and more on my son.

My brother told me more. 'He was hurt in the smash but he'll fully recover.'

'When can I see him?' I tried to say – over and over again!

And at last my brother understood. 'He's still too sick for you to see him, but I'll bring him when he is better.'

Oh my god, the pain! It was getting worse. You were starting to look very worried. Then at the end of one of his sessions with me, I noticed my brother was crying. I wanted to ask him how my son was progressing but I could not make him understand. He went, and I let my boy come flooding back.

We were in the dew-filled field again, just throwing a tennis ball to each other and laughing and fooling around. There was a creek at the end of the field and we ran towards it, throwing the ball to each other as we ran. When we got to the creek, he took his shirt off and jumped in, laughing, and turned and shouted to me, 'Come on, Dad, it's lovely.' But I was slower than him and was having trouble getting my shirt off, while he laughed and splashed and played the fool like a young boy should.

Then I noticed you were wiping my tears again, and you must have given me something because I guess I blacked out.

The next thing I remember – I don't know how long afterwards it was – my brother was with me again. When he saw that I recognised him, he started to speak. I didn't need to read his lips. I could hear him.

'Your son is dead, John. He was killed instantly in the smash. He felt no pain.'

It was about two hours ago that he said that. And I've been dying for two hours. I know the truth, and I'm going to join my son; and my wife too. And all your training and your equipment will only serve to delay the process. You bastards. What's the point in keeping me alive? Let me go. Just leave those damned instruments alone, you bastards. Help me get my shirt off so I can join my son. That creek looked so inviting with him laughing and splashing in it.

I Believe

I didn't particularly like Brett Stacey when he first joined the club. He had a self-confident air that somehow put me off. You'd think that a new member would be a bit diffident at first, but he seemed to know his way around right from the start.

What really annoyed me, however, was the fact that he won what seemed to be more than his fair share of prizes. There were even whispers among the guys of cheating; but I wouldn't have gone that far.

We're only a small club, usually about a dozen or fifteen taking part each week, so it's almost inevitable that sooner or later you're going to finish in the top three in a race. If you're so good that you start winning all the time, you're strongly encouraged (some would say 'instructed') to join one of the bigger clubs in the city. In other words, to move up a grade and leave us to our own comfortable small town ways.

Stacey was almost at that stage, but he seemed happy to stay just below that watermark. Perhaps he was a small-time pot hunter, content to place in the top half-dozen every week rather than have to fight it out with the big boys in the city. If that was the case, it was another reason for me to disapprove of him.

The guys were rightly suspicious because on our regular Wednesday night training runs he would struggle along with the rest of us scrubbers. I've even found him gasping next to me on occasion. But come Sunday morning, I became used to seeing his backside getting further and further ahead of me as the race went on.

Because of the vague whispers amongst the guys that he might be cheating, and also because I've only won one race and got one third place in three years of racing, I decided to try and find out the secret of his success – whether it was legal or not.

What made me doubtful that he could be cheating outright is that there are virtually no rewards for it in our club. A hastily scribbled certificate, a handshake from the secretary, a spattering of applause from the guys after the race, and a medal at the annual dinner. Big deal. If you've found an illegal way of winning, surely you can use it to better advantage than that.

I was finding it hard to think of a way to approach him about his successes when a stroke of fortune came my way.

He started dating my sister.

Angela and I have always been good friends. She's six years older than me, same as Brett, and that's just enough distance so that we weren't sibling rivals but were close enough to share common ground, so to speak. She's not a runner, she's a violinist. And like me, she's not disgraceful but she's no great shakes. She plays sometimes with the small orchestra in the city, but if they're playing a piece that doesn't need so many violins, she's one of the first to get dropped. Nevertheless, she enjoys her music and I approve of it – the same as she approves of my running.

As I said, we get on well together, and when he started dating her, I saw perhaps an opportunity to get to know his secret, if he had one.

She seemed happy with him and he started attending her practice sessions with the orchestra and then a couple of her concerts. And gradually I noticed a change coming over her. I don't think it was love – although I'm not experienced enough in that sphere to comment expertly – but her playing seemed to be improving markedly. There was a sweetness in the tone of that violin that hadn't been there before. The timing seemed more precise and there was a feel of confidence that even my inexpert ear could pick up. And apparently the orchestra officials thought so too, because she was kept in the orchestra for the next piece, which only required six violins overall.

Now, I may not be the brightest star in the sky, but I'm not totally stupid. Something was going on, and Brett Stacey was behind it. It seemed as though it was more than just a straightforward physical boost that a drug might give you for running. His 'secret' seemed to run to the improvement of dexterous skills too.

I couldn't very well say to him, 'Tell me what drug you're using – if you're using one!' so I thought I'd try a bit of detective work on Angela.

I dropped a few broad hints that I'd noticed a marked improvement in her playing since she'd been with Brett. But she wasn't biting. She knew what I was up to – she's cleverer than me – and she would just smile knowingly and say nothing. But she was clearly implying that I should get my knowledge from Brett himself.

Well, as I said, I never particularly liked him, although I was softening towards him a bit because he was being good to my sister, and I found it hard to speak to him about this thing that was worrying me so much. I did manage a few pertinent remarks in conversation, but all I got from him was that same sort of smile that Angela had given me. A smile that said, 'I know a secret and you don't.'

Then came the Sunday morning of the Hillcrest race. An eight-kilometre race that takes in the two steepest hills around our town. Generally regarded as one of the toughest in the calendar.

I'm not very good on hills and I wasn't expecting to shine at all. I was sitting in the car before the race, putting my shoes on, when Brett suddenly opened the door and slipped into the passenger seat.

He looked me straight in the eye and for once he wasn't smiling. 'Drink this,' he said, and offered me a small container of cloudy looking liquid.

'What is it?'

He didn't answer, he just tapped the side of his nose: the universal signal that says, 'Keep quiet about it. It's a secret.'

Then he was gone.

For a few seconds, I wondered whether to drink it or not. I'm a basically honest person but here was my great opportunity to solve the mystery of Brett Stacey and his successes. And, I thought, just once won't do any harm.

I drank it.

Well, I didn't win that race and I didn't get in the top three. But I came fourth, ahead of Brett himself, and surprised everybody including me.

The only explanation I could offer to the guys was that it had been 'Just one of those days when everything goes right.'

But I knew differently, of course.

Brett wouldn't tell me what was in that drink even though I asked him outright the next time I saw him. He just smiled and said, 'You did well.'

It infuriated me.

Whatever it was had done me good and I wanted to do it again. I was sliding into temptation but I figured that a couple of placings in the races would be enough. Then I would stop.

The next week, I waited for him to give me the potion, but he didn't. He treated me quite normally before the race but there was no sign of the drink. I came where I usually come – in the slower half of the pack, and after the race I walked dejectedly back to the car.

'Not so good today, eh?' said Brett, walking beside me.

I looked at him with distaste. He had come third.

'Did you take your drink?' I asked sullenly.

'Sometimes I don't need to,' he said as he departed for his car.

The arrogance! I almost felt like dobbing him in there and then, but I realised I would be compromising myself too if I did that. I was getting myself into a fine pickle.

I thought that if I could get hold of some of his drink I could get it analysed. I didn't know how to go about that: I suppose a chemist might have done it. I couldn't very well take it to an athletics official seeing that I'd had some myself before a race.

But I was saved the trouble in just about the most traumatic way possible.

The next Sunday, Brett suddenly appeared in my car again and just left a container of the drink for me. He didn't say a thing. I figured that he was covering himself. He could always say, 'I didn't tell him to drink it.'

I did drink it but I saved a little bit to take for future analysis.

The race was a longer one, twelve kiliometres including some bush trails, with the finish only visible for the last hundred metres after a sharp corner. I was running really well, lying third and catching the second man. We rounded the final corner together and I gathered up my strength to get in front of him. I raised my eyes to focus on the finish line ready for the final sprint. And nearly fainted from fright.

The greenshirts!

The greenshirts are the national athletic drug testers; they can descend on any race whatsoever in the country to test the runners for illegal drugs. There are lots of them around and just about every club, sooner or later, are going to get a visit from them. No one, not even the officials, know when they are going to appear. And they always do it after the race has started so that any guilty runners have no chance of backing out beforehand.

They were waiting at the finish line for us.

I stumbled and slowed and the other runner passed me to take second place. That was the least of my worries! Up until then, I'd been feeling great. Now my life was about to be ruined.

It wasn't just the disgrace of being found to have taken illegal drugs. In a small town like ours, word would get around and I would be ostracised from everything for the rest of my life. I would quite possibly get the sack from work. I would have to leave, go away altogether, give up any sort of sport once my name was on the blacklist, and live a totally different sort of life.

And I didn't want that.

A greenshirt took a quick sample of my blood – just a painless needle in the arm – and informed me that results would be available in about twenty minutes.

I wondered if Brett had taken his drink this week. But when he came in and was tested he didn't seem concerned at all. I wondered if he knew the greenshirts were going to come and had deliberately set me up.

I felt physically sick, and it wasn't from the effort I'd put into the race.

I had to hang around for the official presentation, having come third, and I'm sure I was the unhappiest third place-getter in the history of the club. Soon the truth would be out. I would have to resign immediately. But the worst part would be the walk back to my car under the glaring eyes of my club mates after I'd been exposed as a drug cheat. I was literally trembling in my shoes.

A couple of the guys came up to me and offered congratulations. 'You're improving,' they said.

I managed a weak smile and glanced guiltily to where the greenshirts were.

Or where the greenshirts should have been.

But they were saying goodbye to the officials, shaking hands and smiling – and then they climbed into their van and were gone.

'No drugs today,' called the secretary jauntily. 'See you all next week.'

I have never felt so weak in the knees as I did just then. I shuffled back to the car, blaming the effort of the race for my slowness, but I just sat there and couldn't drive.

What was going on? Had Brett Stacey found a new drug that the greenshirts couldn't detect? But if so, why was he hanging around a small club like ours? Why wasn't he making money by winning races in the big city? It didn't make sense.

All the other cars had gone. I sat alone in my car, feeling miserable and confused. Then Brett's car sped up, stopped beside me, and suddenly he was in my passenger seat again.

'Good race today, John,' he said. 'You're getting better.'

It was no good. I had to have it out with him. 'What's going on?' I asked, almost savagely. 'What's in that drink? And how come the greenshirts couldn't detect it?'

He looked at me with the eyes of someone who has all the knowledge in the world. 'Nothing's in that drink,' he said. 'Nothing but a mix of a couple of energy drinks that you can buy in any sports store.'

'But...'

'But you thought it was something else, didn't you? And when you drank it, you ran a good race. See, John, your most important running muscle isn't your legs, or your heart, or your lungs. It's inside there!' And he tapped me lightly on the temple. 'That's where your strength lies. That's where everybody's strength lies.'

I was quiet then. He was right, of course. Like many other sportsmen, I had paid attention to my muscles, to my cardiovascular system, to my diet and to my equipment. And I had neglected the most important thing of all: my mind.

One more thing puzzled me. 'What about Angela?' I asked. 'Surely you didn't give her a sports drink to make her a better musician?'

He grinned. 'No. But I used the same principle. I gave her some exercises and told her they were specific ones that Paganini used to use, to make him the great violinist that he was. I said that Paganini used to go through them every morning and that if she did the same, she would be bound to improve.'

'And did Paganini really use those exercises?'

He grinned again as he prepared to climb out of the car. 'Does it matter? Angela believed. She believed, just like you. And she's the better musician for it.'

I had one last question. 'Does she know the truth now?'

'Yes, she does. And she still practises those exercises every morning. She doesn't care whether Paganini used them or not. She realises the problem was all in her head. Same as you.' He climbed into his car and disappeared.

And at last I had the strength to drive home.

That was all about three months ago. I have done well in our races since then, and I know the committee is considering advising me to move up to a city club. It will mean more travelling, of course, but the stiffer competition will only do me good.

I have, however, one more project on the horizon before any of that happens. You see, Brett and Angela got engaged a little while ago and they have already set the wedding date. And Brett has asked me to be his best man. Previously I would have quailed at the thought of having to stand up and give a public speech. But now it doesn't worry me. I know I can do it. I believe.

In the Running

You've all heard of Tubby Wilson, of course. Unless you've been living on another planet these last few years. Sometimes it's hard to pick up a newspaper without mention of him in it somewhere.

His real name is Eric but nobody calls him that. It was me who first called him Tubby, actually, on account of the fact that when he was young he was a bit overweight. And although he's as skinny as a rake these days, the nickname has stuck. That's my claim to fame, I guess.

I've known him all my life. We started school together at the age of five and became friends for no other reason than we were assigned to sit next to each other in class. Of such casual decisions are our lives moulded.

Then when I found that he lived in the next street to me it became a natural thing for me to hang around with him. Or more accurately, for him to hang around with me. In those early days, I was the more dominant one.

There was nothing wrong with Tubby. He was round-faced, round-featured, affable, soft, slow, bland, and totally unremarkable. The type of kid you would forget inside five minutes. Even the school bullies ignored him, on the subconscious grounds that he would provide them with no fun.

He did all right at school – same as me – without being outstanding. We knocked about, did all the things that kids do together, and I was the only friend he had. Not that he had any enemies: he wasn't the type.

We left primary school and went to the same local high school, and I broadened my range of friends. Tubby tagged along with me. And yes, you've guessed it: he was accepted and tolerated but hardly noticed. As I said, he was that kind of kid.

When it came time to leave school, I decided to go to TAFE to learn to become an electrician. Tubby wanted to be a plumber. So we ended up at the same TAFE college.

Life was getting to be more fun. We were old enough to drive, to smoke, to drink, to belch and fart in public, and generally raise hell in our own small town way. We thought we were great boyos. Or at least I did. Tubby went along for the ride as much as he dared but it was obvious his heart wasn't in it.

Then it hit him.

Girls!

Well, one girl to be exact. Her name was Rachel. She was a student at the same college, learning hairdressing, and Tubby – well, to say he fell in love is a gross understatement. He absolutely plummeted in love! Head over heels, as they say. I've never seen anyone so infatuated in my life. And she was a nice girl, too. Good-looking, nice figure, and with a pleasant personality. Down to earth, cheerful, and not snobbish in any way. Not a party-going rager but a sensible, intelligent girl.

Just the type for Tubby.

There was only one problem. She already had a boyfriend. Or at least, a guy she was very interested in. Which made it hard for Tubby.

I gleaned all this from conversations with the hairdressing girls. Tubby's plumbers were way over the other side of campus, but we electrical students were on the same floor as the hairdressers and we would chat regularly. I found out a lot about her for him. Well, he was my mate, wasn't he? And he still is, even though I don't see much of him nowadays.

I had to be careful, of course. I couldn't just walk up to her and say, 'Tell me all about yourself because my mate fancies you.' I had to get into casual conversation with the girls, let on I was a bit interested in some of them (not too far from the truth!), and try to steer the talk around to Rachel to see if I could find out anything more about her for my old mate Tubby.

Thus it was that I was able to report to him one day that the guy she was interested in was going to be running in a marathon in three months' time and that she would be ecstatic if he won.

For the first time in my life I saw a light of determination and purpose in Tubby's eyes.

'Running, eh!' he said. 'I'll find out where he's running and beat him. Then maybe she'll take notice of me!'

I had to suppress a laugh, but I couldn't help saying it. 'You can't run. You were no good at school and you've not done any exercise since.'

But he had that look again. 'I've got to try,' he said. 'Will you help me?'

Of course I'd help him. He was my mate, wasn't he? My best mate, in fact. But I didn't realise what this running gig entailed.

Tubby was at my door at six o'clock the next morning, already warmed up and ready to go. 'Get in the car,' he said, 'and follow me. I want you to tell me when I've done ten k and tell me how long it took.'

Well, I can tell you now, it took him a long time! As I've said, Tubby was soft and slow, and ten k is a long way to run when you've never done it before. I honestly thought he was going to end up in hospital that day, but he finished it, red-faced, sweating, gasping, and sprawled on the ground with his head on his arms for ten minutes afterwards.

No girl was worth that much, I reckoned. 'That's the end of it, then,' I said as we drove back.

'What!?' he said.

'Surely you're not going on with it after that.'

He looked at me as though I'd just declared World War III. 'See you tomorrow morning at six o'clock,' he said, and there was a new tone in his voice that I'd never heard before.

So you could say, then, that I was Tubby Wilson's first coach. If following him in the car every morning and picking him up half-dead at the end could be called coaching. And when the weekend came, he wanted to go on a long run. A long run! Wasn't ten k long enough?

'No. A marathon's forty-two k. I've got to build up to that.'

Ah well, he was my mate. I brought along drinks, food, energy bars and all that sort of thing for him. And day after day, week after week, he ran.

He began to change noticeably. He lost that softness. He lost that affable easy-going bearing. Became more determined. Hard. And he lost weight. Became downright skinny. And instead of asking me to do things, he started telling me. Not in a nasty way, mind, but he was building strength of character and it was starting to show.

'Perhaps you should go in a couple of races beforehand to see how you go,' I said one day.

'No,' he replied. 'I don't want that guy to know I'm going to be a rival.'

We'd seen that guy. The guy Rachel was interested in. Tall, goofy, with not an ounce of fat on him. Buck teeth and going bald.

'What does she see in him?' asked Tubby miserably the first time we saw him.

'Well, he's no great looker,' I said. 'But maybe he can run fast.'

Tubby gave the guy a look of pure hatred. 'As from tomorrow, I'm doubling the distance of my runs.'

I figured that if he wasn't going to run in a race before the big day, then at least I could find out if his times were likely to worry our goofy adversary. I got hold of some race results and compared them to the times Tubby had been doing on his recent training runs. And what I found there nearly made my hair stand on end.

Tubby was good. In fact, he was very good! So good that it scared me. If he could do times like that in training after only a few weeks, what could he do with a couple of years of solid work under his belt? The guy was potential Olympic standard! Of course, you all know that now. But as I said, it scared me then, because I knew that I wasn't old enough, wasn't experienced enough, wasn't good enough to be the coach of someone with that amount of talent. And he would walk over Goofy, that was for sure.

Now one problem that I have, which I don't like to publicise too much, is that I'm a bit hard of hearing. I was born that way. I don't have to wear a hearing aid or anything, and I get by with a bit of lip reading and concentrating harder than normal. But I still make the occasional mistake.

And when the big day drew closer I spoke to Rachel and said, 'How do you think your friend will go in the race?' A bit of detective work for my mate Tubby, see.

'Race?' she said. 'What do you mean?'

'That guy you like. You think he'll win the marathon?'

Not with Tubby in it, he won't, I thought.

'What makes you think he's running in a marathon?'

The seeds of panic started sprouting in my gut. 'Ages ago,' I said, 'you reckoned he was going to be running in a marathon on the fifteenth and that he could win.'

She looked at me blankly for a moment and then started to laugh. 'Oh no,' she said. 'You must have heard me wrong. I said he was in the running to win the annual marathon chess championship on the fifteenth. They play for twelve hours non-stop. And he could win.'

Hell's bells and buckets of blood! What had I done! I'd got it all wrong and fed my best mate false information and put him through all that agony. And all to no avail. A marathon is a running race of forty-two kilometres. Nothing else. But you hear people talk of marathon parliamentary debates, marathon tennis matches, marathon this and marathon that. And now a marathon chess tournament of all things!

I cursed my stupidity and my poor hearing. And I trembled to think what Tubby would say when I plucked up the courage to tell him that Goofy wasn't a runner but a chess player.

'Goofy?' he said. 'Don't worry about him. The man I'm concerned about is Ray Coulson. He's good. He's won a couple of marathons and he's the favourite to win this one. But I'll stick with him and burn him off in the last few ks.'

'You have changed,' I said. That was the understatement of the year. 'But what about Rachel?'

He shrugged. 'Perhaps she deserves Goofy. Now let's get going. I want to do twenty hard ks today.'

And that, ladies and gentlemen, is how Tubby Wilson got started on his stellar career. You know the rest, of course. Olympic Games gold medal; Commonwealth Games gold medal; world champion; world record. Just about every major marathon in the book. Universally acknowledged as the greatest long distance runner this country has ever produced. And only last month, selected to be the captain of our athletics squad in the next Olympic Games. You know all that.

The last time I saw Tubby before he went away for professional training, he was running along the road with a girl. She was attractive, fit, slim, and obviously a good runner. Just the type for Tubby. They were laughing and chatting as they ran, and it was plain even to me that they were more than just training partners.

We still keep in casual contact. Tubby sends me a Christmas card and I do likewise. Or I should say, we do likewise. The two of us. And – just to let you into a little secret – soon to be the three of us, if you get my drift.

You see, after Tubby won that first marathon and decided he needed a proper coach, I sat down and worked out what I really wanted out of life. Tubby had shown me that hard work and dedicated practice brought results. So in every spare minute I got after that, I studied and I practised hard. I followed Tubby's example. I got up early and by six o'clock I had my head down, applying myself. I didn't waste a minute. I became single-minded. I had only one purpose.

And the following year I beat Goofy in the annual marathon chess tournament.

Yes, we send Tubby the regular Christmas card. Rachel and I.

The Catalyst

We decided to hike around the Big Island that holiday. The islands of Hawaii consist of six main islands: Oahu, on which is the city of Honolulu where my wife and I were students, Molokai, Kauai, Maui, Lanai, and the island from which the whole group takes its name: Hawaii. The island of Hawaii, with an area of four thousand square miles, is the largest of them all, and is often affectionately referred to as the Big Island. Even so, my wife and I decided we could walk around it comfortably in the time available to us.

But we had not bargained for injuries. After eight days, she developed a blister on her heel. It grew worse, rubbing against her shoe. She tried walking barefoot, but that failed to release the tight pain of the blister. We were nearly three-quarters of the way round the island and had plenty of time to spare, so when it got so bad that she could hardly walk, we headed for the nearest park.

'A couple of days' rest and you'll be as good as new,' I assured her.

'We'll see,' she said. 'The blister's burst now. I just hope it doesn't get infected.'

We walked into the park and looked around. It was going to have to be our home for at least a couple of days. It was quiet, away from the main road, and a little run-down, but we saw toilets and showers and decided it would do. The sea lapped at the park's edge, but the absence of a good beach in a land where beaches are all-important ensured that it would never become popular.

There were a couple of pavilions – tin roofs mounted on poles about ten feet high, with a concrete floor and a barbecue and chairs; but one of the pavilions was piled high with garbage, while under the other sat four or five seedy, run-down-looking men.

'The local bums,' I said. 'Harmless enough, probably. We'll pitch our tent over there.'

We pitched the tent and rested. We were close enough to the bums to hear them talk but far enough away to converse privately to each other in low tones.

We were tired. The Hawaiian sun can be merciless when you're walking under it all day. After a while, we lit a fire and boiled some water, and my wife bathed her foot.

'Aloha,' came a voice above us. 'You got troubles?' It was one of the bums. He was tall and rangy with dark wavy hair, and the constant outdoor living had bronzed and dried his skin. But I guessed he was not much older than me. About thirty.

'I've burst a blister on my foot,' said my wife. 'I think it's getting infected.'

'Let's have a look.'

I watched anxiously as he took her foot in his hand and peered at it.

He seemed to sense my concern. He looked at me and smiled. 'It's getting infected all right,' he said, 'but you've caught it early. If you bathe it in hot salt water as often as you can, you'll prob'ly fix it in two or three days.'

I nodded in thanks. The ice had been broken.

'Name's Don,' he said.

'Pete,' I introduced myself. Then, 'You seem to know how to cure things.' It was as much a question as a statement.

'I like doing that sort of thing,' he said. 'The boys call me Doctor Don. I fix up their scratches and bruises and concoct drinks to settle their upset stomachs. Stuff like that.' He seemed almost embarrassed saying it and quickly changed the subject. 'What y'r doin' here anyway?'

'We're Australians,' I said. 'Students in Honolulu. We decided to hike around the island during our semester break.'

'Get far?'

'Almost all the way. Looks like we're stuck here for a few days now, though.'

He grinned. 'Come on over and I'll introduce you to the boys.'

'The boys' turned out to be quite a decent bunch. They were all much older than Don and showed instant friendliness towards us, although I sensed that their friendliness came from the philosophy that it was too much trouble to be antagonistic toward us, or to anyone. It was a weak sort of friendship, but then they were weak sort of men: not physically but psychologically, in their dealings with each other and with other people.

Don, although the youngest, seemed to be the natural leader of the group. His closest friend was a thick-set, nasal-voiced man called Carl, who delighted in telling us stories of his escapades when he was a truck driver in California. Then there was a man known as Fergie, the oldest of them all, who told me over and over again that the Australians were the finest fighting men in the history of warfare. Earl was a fat, belching man who hardly spoke all night but just sat and listened with a weak smile; while the other man, called Johnny, left us halfway through the evening to drive into town.

'Gone to the movies again,' grinned Carl.

'He goes to the movies every night,' Don told us.

'How does he afford it?'

'He doesn't pay. He just cleans up for them afterwards. It saves them paying someone the proper wages. Ol' Johnny knows a film off by heart by the end of the week.'

Don himself had apparently lived all his life in Hawaii. He told us he had once been married but his wife had divorced him. Now he didn't care any more, he said. He was happy as he was.

We talked of this and that and the time passed pleasantly, but the conversation never grew deep. They spoke freely and at length about their past lives, but never any plans for the future, and never about us. Our job was to listen, because we were a new and virtually a captive audience, but we listened well, having grown accustomed to that in college, and the bums seemed pleased with us. Shallow men, then, I thought, well-meaning and harmless, but weak and without ambition. They seemed totally content in what they were.

Was this, I thought, what the human race was headed for? As we strive and achieve more and more things, perhaps one day we will find we have achieved everything, and be satisfied and content – and thus develop the characteristics of these men. Did they represent, then, the peak of human development? Absurd, I chuckled to myself…and so my thoughts drifted lazily as we sat and listened to their stories.

The warm Hawaiian evening breeze brushed against our cheeks. A full moon rose and glimmered on the peaceful sea.

'No wonder they call them the enchanted isles,' I said.

'It gets you after a while,' smiled Don. 'If you stay here too long, you get so you don't want to do anything. You just want to enjoy the beauty of the place.'

We retired early that night. A long walk and the striking up of new friendships can be tiring experiences, and we drifted to sleep with the sound of the men's voices in our ears, and the constant muffled boom of the surf in the background.

*

When we woke the next morning, there was a new voice. I lay and listened to make sure. Yes, there was Don, there was Carl's nasal twang, there was Fergie's rough growl, Johnny trying to talk about last night's film, and even Earl got in a few words. But there was a new voice. It had a definite southern accent and seemed lighter and somehow more vigorous than the others.

He – whoever it was – was telling them about how he had once persuaded a judge to release a man so that he could work for him. 'So I said, "Look, jedge, if y' put him in jail, y' gotta feed him and pay someone t' look after him. Why don' y' let him go and he c'n come an' work f'r me – that way I'll be happy an' you'll be better off."

'"Why're you so anxious t' have him released?" says the jedge.

'"Well, jedge," says I, "he's the bes' worker I ever seen. He's worth two men to me."

'"Well, I guess that's okay," says the jedge, an' he lets him go.'

I opened the flap of the tent, just a little, to see who the owner of this voice was. It was a compact, neat man with close-cropped hair and a ruddy face. He was sitting on the table with his feet on the bench, and the warm sun shone full on his face from its low angle. If I had been a painter, I could have used the setting to depict a modern Hawaiian Christ preaching to his disciples, except for the fact that no one was listening to him. The men were lighting cigarettes, washing their breakfast plates, commenting among themselves and generally fidgeting around, with the air of people who have heard it all before but don't want to appear impolite.

I closed the flap and turned back to my wife. 'How's the foot?' I whispered.

'Throbbing,' she said, and snuggled up to kiss me. 'But otherwise I'm very healthy.'

When we woke again a little later, the new voice had gone. We dressed and washed and then strolled over to meet the boys.

'Thought you were going to sleep all day.'

I smiled, perhaps a little sheepishly, and started to prepare some salt water for her foot. But Don was ahead of me and came forward with everything ready to bathe the blister. I remembered then that his nickname amongst the men was Doctor Don. He certainly had the enthusiasm, and no small talent, to truly earn his appellation. He was rather quiet as he went about his work and I had noticed the look he had given us when we had emerged from the tent. I knew that he had guessed why we were so late in rising. I remembered he had been married once and I wondered, after seeing that look, if he really was as content as he made out. The others no doubt had also guessed in their crude way what we had been doing in the tent, but Don's perception had gone deeper and I sensed that underneath the crust of indifference that he had chosen to wear, here was a sensitive man.

'I thought I heard somebody else with you this morning,' I said.

'Oh, that was Megga,' said Don.

'Who?'

'Megga. He comes here regular. He's a house painter. Quite well off. But he likes to come and yarn to us. Sometimes he offers us work but we don't accept very often.'

'If Megga's offering work, I wouldn't mind doing a couple of days,' I said. 'We could use the money and we can't move anyway until the blister heals. When will Megga come again?'

'Probably tonight. I'm surprised he wasn't here yesterday. He usually comes most days.'

'Where does he live?'

'In town.'

'Why does he come here if he's got his own business and a house in town?'

Don shrugged. 'Perhaps he hates his wife. Perhaps he just likes to talk. Who knows? Who cares?'

Don may have been a good amateur doctor but he was a poor amateur actor. I sensed immediately that there was more to it than that.

'He's useful, though,' volunteered Carl. 'If the cops start hassling us, Megga comes and bails us out. And we can always do a day's work for him. Not that that happens very often.'

'He's like a godfather, then?' I said.

They laughed in agreement and Don said, 'If you speak to him tonight, you'll be able to get a couple of days with him. Can you paint?'

'Well enough.'

'Good. I'll go and get some more sea salt for that there wound.' And he set off across the grass towards the rocks, where the Pacific surf pounded endlessly under the hot Hawaiian sun.

*

Megga and I took a liking to each other straight away.

'Right,' he said when I put forward my proposition. 'Start t'morrow. I'll pick y' up here. Seven o'clock. Can y' paint?'

'Painted our house in Australia before we came here,' I said confidently.

'Good 'nough f'r me,' he said. He was different from the other men. He seemed brighter and more purposeful, more energetic, even in just his speech. 'Anybody else wan' a day's work?'

Profound silence answered him, except for Earl, who said, 'No thanks, Megga.'

'Well, at least there's one polite bastard amongst yous,' said Megga cheerfully. Then, 'Did I ever tell y'r about…' and so he was off on another yarn.

They had all heard it before, except for me of course, and that was good enough for Megga. The men gradually drifted into conversation of their own, and Megga ended up speaking just to me. He was a more interesting man. I felt that we could have some good discussions once he had told me all his stories.

After a while, we got round to talking about each other a little. I informed him that I was just an ordinary working man who, together with Colette, had managed to obtain a working scholarship to college in Hawaii.

'It's hard going,' I said, 'trying to study and make a living at the same time.'

'Yeah,' he agreed, ''specially in Hawaii. It's a great place f'r the millionaire tourist, but not so great when y'r jest a battlin' worker.'

'Where do you come from, Megga?'

'Missouri.' He pronounced it Mizzoora.

'What made you come to Hawaii?'

A fleeting, evasive look passed over his face, barely noticeable, but then he grinned. 'Why does anybody come t' Hawaii? It's th' greatest place in th' world, ain't it?'

So his brashness held, and he swung into another of his yarns. But he had not deceived me. Neither he nor the others had asked me, but at college I was studying psychiatry, which, amongst other things, involved studying your fellow man very closely. And I had not missed that split second when his defences had been down, and I had not been fooled for one moment by his evasive and vague answer. There's more to you than meets the eye, Megga, I thought, and you're a damn good actor, but I wonder why you have really settled in Hawaii.

It was getting late. Coffee was made and we all sat around the solid wooden table. The moon was up again.

'Johnny'll be back from the movies soon,' someone said.

'I can't for the life of me,' said Carl, 'see why that silly bastard goes to the movies every night when he can sit and yarn with us and enjoy something like that,' as he pointed to the silver streak the moon made on the water.

'He's an idiot, that's why,' said Fergie. 'A good spell in the army would have straightened him out.'

'Oh, balls about your army,' said Don. 'You reckon that's the answer for everything.'

Megga was sitting opposite me and I could see what he was thinking. An argument was in the making.

'Have yous ever thought,' he said, 'that Johnny might have a girl frien' down there? What about that woman who serves the ice cream?'

A vulgar guffaw greeted his remark. 'Have you seen her? She must be eighteen stone if she's a pound! Ol' Johnny wouldn't go for that!'

'Well,' said Megga, his eyes twinkling – and I knew he had accomplished what he was aiming at – 'ol' Johnny's no oil painting his-self, you know.'

The laughter continued. 'You're goddam right there. Even if he set his cap at her, she'd probably reject him anyway.'

It seemed to be a fine joke for everybody, and the laughter and bawdy remarks were only just beginning to subside when Johnny himself drove into the park. They all started laughing again.

'Hey, listen,' said Megga seriously. 'Don't needle him about it. He might get upset, and he's the only one of yous who's got a car. That's mighty useful at times. Remember that.'

They quietened accordingly and when Johnny came amongst us we greeted him soberly and gave him some coffee, but I noticed Don and Carl turn away to chuckle to themselves, while Earl's constant grin was definitely broader than usual. The laughter was only just under the surface and seemed due to burst out at any time.

Megga moved to control the situation and he did so with admirable neatness. 'Well I'm off now,' he said. 'It's late, guys. See y'all in the mornin'. Get some beauty sleep y'selves – y' need it!'

We chorused our goodbyes and the party immediately broke up. I strolled over to the tent. Blessed are the peacemakers, I thought, especially if they have a southern accent and don't want to say why they settled in Hawaii.

*

Working for Megga proved to be a hectic experience. I had always regarded myself as a fit man, but by lunchtime on that first day I was already beginning to ache. Megga was as nippy in his movements as he was in his appearance. I won't say that he slave-drove me, but he made sure I never had any idle moments. He went flat out himself, and by mid-afternoon we were both absolutely soaked in sweat. We agreed on a ten-minute break, and I knew that Megga would make sure it *was* only ten minutes.

His work was the reflection of the man: good, clean and neat, no frills and absolutely honest. The more I thought about it, the more it seemed that his fraternisation with the park bums was totally out of character. But I remembered what Don had said – 'Perhaps he hates his wife' – and perhaps Megga's home life was a different world again. But then I thought about Don's evasive responses and figured that perhaps he knew more about Megga than he cared to reveal.

We ate in the shade of the half-painted veranda for our quick ten-minute break.

'Why do they call you Megga?' I asked. 'Surely that's not your real first name?'

'Short f'r Meggarity,' he said. 'My first name's Phillip, but I've always been called Megga ever since I was a kid.'

67

'In Mizzoora,' I smiled.

'Yeah,' he laughed.

'Meggarity,' I said. 'That'd be Irish.'

'Yeah. Many generations ago, though. Wife too. She's an O'Sullivan.'

Ah! The first mention of Megga's wife. I tried to think of some appropriate question to learn more of her but I was too slow.

Megga was on his feet. 'Okay, let's get back into it.'

So back into it we got and I had no more chance to speak to him intimately again that day.

When he drove me back to the park, he kept up a constant chatter of his yarns, and to be honest I was too tired to worry about it. But I felt that I had earned my money and I asked him if I could work for him the next day.

'Sure,' he said cheerfully. 'Same time, same place. Let's hope it's a little cooler.' Then he promptly stripped off his shirt and ran into the sea, swimming out strongly before turning to face us.

'Doesn't he ever slow down?' I asked Don, who was fishing off the nearby rocks.

He grinned. 'Now you know why we don't work for him very often.'

Colette limped up and hooked her arm through mine. She said that two more days should see her fit enough for us to move on. We strolled along the water's edge, where the blue Pacific boomed rhythmically, never-ending, seemingly remote and infinite.

'Hey! Hey! Hey! Megga! Megga!'

We whirled. Don was on his feet, fishing rod gone, waving his arms and shouting wildly. 'Megga! Megga! Get in! Get in! There's a shark! Get in!'

I gaped out to see and immediately saw it – that sinister dark fin cutting through the water parallel to the beach. But it was a long way from Megga and didn't appear to be going directly towards him. Nor was it going particularly fast. But Megga didn't know that: he was thrashing wildly towards us.

Don sprinted along the beach toward him. 'Get in, Megga! Get in!'

It only served to make him panic all the more. I could see the naked fear in his eyes.

'Aagh! My leg!' Megga was only a few yards out but his face contorted in pain and he stopped swimming. 'My leg!'

Don jumped into the water and waded out. He was only waist-deep when he grabbed Megga's arm and started to pull him in. The physical contact seemed to calm him. He started to help himself again. They got out of the water and he flopped to the ground.

'My leg! What happened?'

We knelt to look. 'You bashed it against a rock, that's all,' Don said. 'It's bleeding but it's not serious.'

He was definitely the doctor of the outfit. The other men had come, disturbed by the commotion.

I whispered to my wife, 'Slip back and make some coffee. We'll all be over in a couple of minutes.'

'A bad cut,' pronounced Don. 'A bit deep but not serious. You've just got to keep it clean. Can you walk now?'

With a grunt, Megga put his arm on Don's shoulder and raised himself. He put his weight on his injured leg, winced, almost went down, and decided he could make it. We moved slowly back to the pavilion. Megga had his arm on Don's shoulder, and I tried to watch them closely. I do not know why, but the way they conducted themselves told me that there was no homosexual relationship: but there was something there.

'Ah, coffee! Good.'

Megga's knee was bathed and bandaged. His brashness was gone.

'The shark was a long way away,' said Don. 'You thought you'd been bitten because that's what you were expecting. If there'd been no shark, you'd have cursed that rock black and blue.'

'If there'd been no shark, I wouldn't have blundered into it.' But he was quiet and pale. He was in a mild form of shock.

'You ought to get home,' I said. 'Have a good long bath and get your wife to dress your wound again.'

I watched him closely to see what effect my mention of his wife would have. But he seemed to think it was an excellent idea.

'Will you be able to work tomorrow?' I asked.

'I think so. Even if I can't I'll be able to supervise you.' But he said it quietly and soberly. 'Thank you,' he said. 'And thank you especially, Donny boy.' Then he rose and limped to his car without waiting to see Don's reaction.

Don spoke quietly. 'The bastard knows I don't like being called Donny boy.' But he said it affectionately, like someone who has been given champagne when all he had asked for was lemonade.

*

But the events of that day were not yet over. Tired physically from my day's work and tired emotionally from the shark incident, I went to bed early. The men, however, had apparently decided to make a night of it. From the snugness of our tent, we could hear their animated conversation and the frequent click of bottles. I remembered that it was welfare cheque day. Once again they had money, and therefore they had drink.

Colette and I settled into our sleeping blanket and relaxed, but it was impossible to sleep. The men were making too much noise. The shark dominated the conversation for a while, and then I heard the sound of a car driving away.

'There goes Johnny again,' I heard Carl say. 'Off to his fat girlfriend.'

Laughter all round. Bawdy remarks and obscene suggestions were yelled after the disappearing car and I wondered if Johnny heard any of it.

Their talk drifted to other things. Johnny came into the conversation a lot. Now that he was not here, he couldn't defend himself. Obscenities and vulgar laughter. The clink of bottles. Their voices grew louder and more aggressive. Carl's voice was getting slurry already. I heard the sound of someone urinating. A belch and a fart. Then the sound of breaking glass and a string of curses.

My wife trembled and held me close. This was a side of the boys we had not seen. This was why they were bums. I wished Megga was here but the peacemaker was injured. Their talk grew filthier and more aggressive. It was obvious how the night was going to end.

Then, for no apparent reason, they grew quieter. It seemed they had run out of things to say. But as a psychiatric student I judged that it was the lull before the storm. They had had enough of verbal aggression and were waiting for the chance to start on the real thing. It was a bad night.

'Hey.' This was Don. His voice was slurry. 'How long you think it would take me to walk into town an' back?'

'Where in town?'

'The centre. Say the post office.'

'Why?'

'Because I'm a damn fine walker, that's why. How long?'

'Must be three miles to the post office an' three miles back. Six miles. Take you over an hour and a quarter.'

There was a slight pause. Then Don's voice came, presenting his time to them like an artist unveiling his picture. 'Two t'irds of an hour.'

'What!'

'Bullshit!'

'You can't walk to the post office and back in forty minutes!'

'Impossible!'

From the safety and darkness of the tent I had to agree with them. Don would have been hard-pressed to run six miles in forty minutes, let alone walk. But he was speaking again.

'See that stride?' I could picture him stretching his legs. 'That's a hell of a big stride.'

'Impossible,' Fergie was saying. 'Impossible.'

'You couldn't run that fast.' That was Earl.

'I get tired when I run,' said Don. 'But when I walk I get into a rhythm.' And again he said, 'See that stride? That's a hell of a big stride.'

And all the time Fergie kept saying, 'Impossible! Impossible!'

'Two t'irds of an hour,' Don repeated.

'All right, we'll bet on it,' said Fergie.

But Don ignored the offer. 'What time is it, Carl?' he said.

'Just coming up to twenty-five past.'

I heard a swish as someone passed the tent, and then there was silence. Don had obviously started his walk.

'Impossible,' Fergie said again. 'Impossible.'

They grew quiet. The bottles clinked. Someone urinated. I wondered what was going to happen in forty minutes when Don did not return. But how were they going to know if he had gone all the way to the post office? The situation was ridiculous.

I must have dozed off because the next thing I heard was Carl shouting, 'For Chrissake, shut up! We'll know if it's impossible in another two minutes!'

But it made no difference to Fergie. 'Impossible,' he kept saying. 'Impossible.' He would pause for a few moments and then start again. 'Impossible. Impossible.'

The time drifted on.

Fergie was muttering, 'Impossible, impossible,' all the time. I judged the two minutes were up.

'Impossible. Impossible.'

'Shaddap!' Carl yelled at the top of his voice, and my wife jerked out of her sleep.

Fergie was quiet for a little while and then it came again. 'Impossible. Impossible. He's over his forty minutes. I told you it was impossible.'

'How do you know he's over his forty minutes?' yelled Carl, and I heard a sharp clatter and then a confused thump.

'Something's happened to him. I'm going to see!'

I heard Carl walk past and his sound faded away. Fergie was muttering to himself, his voice thick and slurry.

'There was no need for that.' A heavy breath. 'I may be an old man…' A heavy breath. 'I may be an old man but I'm no coward.' A heavy breath. 'I'll kill him!'

Some more heavy breathing. Then again, 'I may be an old man but I'm no coward. I'll kill the bastard!'

'Oh, be quiet Fergie.' This was Earl. There was only him and Fergie left.

'I'll kill him! I may be an old man but I'm no coward.' A pause. Then, 'I'll kill the bastard!'

I heard a clatter and a stumble, and a thump as a body hit the ground. Fergie had obviously collapsed in a drunken stupor.

'Stupid bastard,' Earl was saying. 'Stupid bastard.'

Then there was silence, except for the ever-present sound of the surf pounding on the rocks.

*

Megga's knee was swollen the next morning but he was able to limp around and do his work.

'Boys had a wild time las' night, did they?' he grinned.

'They sure did,' I said. 'Laid themselves out. How did you know?'

'It was welfare cheque day. They always do that.'

I was about to ask him why on earth he associated with them, but he started with instructions on how to erect a small scaffold and we immediately concentrated on that. When we had it constructed, he grabbed his brush and pot and started up the ladder.

'Megga,' I said, 'don't you think you ought to stay on the ground with your knee.'

'I'll be okay,' he replied. 'I ain't goin' to let a little cut worry me.'

It might not have worried Megga but it worried me. I was immediately underneath him as he worked on the scaffold, and I was getting splashed with paint. 'Hey, Megga, be careful! You're turning me yellow!'

He laughed. 'You frightened of becoming a Chinaman, Pete? Ha ha. Aagh!' Yellow paint poured over me and Megga crashed to the ground. 'Aagh!'

'Jeez, Megga, are you all right?'

'I've broke m' ankle, I'm sure I have. Oh, hell!'

'Don't move, Megga. I'll get help!'

*

The doctor at the hospital smiled at me. 'Well, Mr Yellowman, I see you've got cleaned up. Your friend is better than you thought. All he's got is a badly sprained ankle and a few bruises. We've dressed his knee too, and given him something to relax him.'

'It was his knee that caused it,' I said. 'He cut it yesterday and it went on him today.'

'Yes. Well, a couple of days in bed and he'll be as good as new. You can take him home now. You'll find he's still a bit wonky from the drug.'

I got Megga into his car and jumped into the driver's seat. 'I hope you're well enough to tell me how to get to your house,' I said.

He nodded weakly. Suddenly he seemed a lot smaller. I wondered if I was going to get to the bottom of the mystery of this man. At least I was going to have the chance to meet his wife.

Megga's wife was beautiful. Not in a Miss Universe way, but in a comfortable, you're-the-girl-I-want-to-marry sort of way. She was very quiet, a good listener, but serene and poised. I got the impression that she knew Megga inside out. I explained what had happened, and we put him to bed. I prepared to go, but Megga motioned me to stay. His wife kissed him and went out. She had understood instinctively that he wanted to be alone with me.

Megga's eyes were moist and a little glazed. The effects of the drug were obviously still on him. 'Guess I can't offer you any more work,' he said.

'That's okay, Megga. Colette's foot is almost better. We'll probably be moving on tomorrow.'

He was silent for a little while. Then he seemed to come to a decision. 'You're an intelligent man,' he said, 'and an observant man. You've wondered why I go to the park.'

I nodded. 'Yes.'

He wasn't looking at me. His eyes were still moist. 'I love my wife. You've seen how good she is. I love her. Only trouble is, she can't have any chil'ren.'

I said nothing. The seconds ticked away. He glanced over at me. 'That's why I go to th' park.'

I frowned. 'I don't understand.'

'They're the only family I've got. They're my boys.'

'But most of them are older than you.'

'They're still boys. You saw that last night. They're like a family. They fight. They make up. They bitch. They laugh at each other's expense. But they never break up.'

'And they'll never grow up,' I said. Then I paused. 'Except perhaps for Don. He's still young enough to change. He's too young to be a bum.'

'He's been a bum all his life,' said Megga.

'But he was married once.'

'D'you know how long that lasted? Three weeks. He was a bum before he was married an' he was a bum three weeks later.'

There was silence for a few moments.

It was now or never, I thought. 'Why are you so interested in Don?' I said.

He said nothing for a while, and the question hung in the air. Then his mouth opened. 'He's my son.'

'What!?'

'He's my son. I'm his father.'

'B-b-but – but he's too old!'

'He's thirty-one. I'm forty-six.' He looked at me. 'It is possible to become a father at fifteen, you know.'

'Yes, but…'

He interrupted me. 'I was at school. There was this – this high school whore, that's th' only thing I c'n call her. She seduced me. Then she told me she was havin' my kid. I said we'd get married, even though I detested her by then. But she said no. She said she was goin' to Hawaii, was goin' to be a prostitute.'

He swallowed hard and then continued. 'Well, I was fifteen. A poor boy f'm Missouri. I couldn't afford t' come here. I was twenty-one before I made it. I found her. She was a prostitute in Honolulu. When she knew I was here, she disappeared. Then I was drafted into th' army. When I got back it was the same ol' story. She didn't want me to see my son. Not that she ever cared for him. He had a rough upbringing. She was changin' addresses every few weeks, getting' harassed by the cops, getting' beaten up by clients, getting' hassled by pimps. Don never had a chance. But she kept him away f'm me. And she got help f'm the underworld. I was threatened with my life more than once. The boy grew up not knowing who his father was.'

'Does he know now?'

'No.'

'Why don't you tell him?'

'Don't y' see? He hates his father. Or at least, he hates the image of his father that his mother gave him. If he was to find out that good ol' Megga was his dad, well…' His voice trailed off.

'So,' I said, 'you're acting the part of his father – and to all the group – to make up for all those lost years.'

He nodded weakly. 'Something like that.'

I leaned forward. 'But don't you see, Megga, that if you don't tell him, he'll never change. At least give him the chance: give him an identity. When he's got over the shock, he'll realise he's got a father to be proud of.'

'No,' he said. 'No. He's condemned to the life of a bum. How c'n you know what it's like to be brought up by a two-bit whore who doesn't care for you? Don couldn't be anything else. Besides, he's happy. If he tried t' change, it would shatter him. An' what father wants t' see his son unhappy?'

Suddenly he gripped my arm. 'Promise me one thing,' he said.

I nodded vigorously. He was hurting my arm.

'Don't tell him. Or anyone. You're goin' tomorrow. I've told you in confidence. I know I c'n trust you.'

'Okay,' I said. 'Okay. You'd better get some sleep now.'

But Megga's eyes were already closed and his breathing was heavy and regular.

*

'There's something doesn't gel somewhere,' I said as I recounted the story to my wife. I guessed I was safe telling her.

'Yes,' she said, 'and I'll tell you what it is. I've seen more of the boys than you have, being here all day. And Don is different from the others. He's sensitive, or he could be if he gave himself the chance. I do agree with Megga that he's happy here. But I don't agree that he's condemned to the life of a bum. He could be something more if he wanted to. He just doesn't want to. He is completely happy as he is.'

'No,' I said. 'He misses the love of a woman.'

'He goes to the local brothel. He told me.'

'I don't mean that. I mean – well, you know, companionship, intimacy, that sort of thing.'

'But he gets that with Megga.'

'It's not the same. And he doesn't know Megga's his father.'

'He doesn't have to. Megga's like a godfather – to all of them. That's good enough for Don.'

'I'm not convinced,' I said. 'But what's for tea?'

'What if we go into town and have a meal?' she said. 'I don't want to spend another night like last night.'

I nodded. The boys were sure to have some drink left. 'Yes. We'll have a meal and go to the movies. Then we can get a lift back with Johnny.'

'Good.'

It had been another hot day, and even in the evening it was still warm enough for us to wear light clothing, and saunter round the few attractions of the small town.

'I'm glad we're leaving tomorrow,' said my wife. 'I'm ready for a change of scenery again. And the boys were different today. I think they felt ashamed in front of me.'

'Life is never as simple as it seems,' I said, lost in my own thoughts. 'I wish I could make Megga see that he's holding Don back by not telling him who he is.'

'Come on, relax while you've got the chance,' she said. 'We're back to our studies very shortly. Let's enjoy the meal and the film. What is it, by the way?'

'A comedy.'

'Good. Just what you need.'

That was true. It did relax me. I even had a quiet chuckle when I caught sight of Johnny's supposed girlfriend in the intermission. She was huge.

Colette chastised me. 'Remember we're getting a lift back with him tonight. Don't offend him.'

But Johnny was not easily offended. I had no idea if he knew about the boys' remarks concerning himself and the ice cream girl; but if he did, it didn't worry him. He was in a talkative mood as we drove back to the park. He asked us how we liked Hawaii, how we had enjoyed our stay in the park, and how Megga was. 'You and him seemed to get along pretty well,' he said.

'Yes,' I said. 'We became good mates.'

He was silent for a few moments, then, 'I suppose he told you he was Don's father.'

I stared, speechless. I swallowed. 'How did you know?'

'Oh, we all know,' he chuckled.

'Even Don?'

'Yeah. Even Don. Known it for years.'

Now I was totally confused. 'But – does Megga know that Don knows?'

'No. He thinks nobody knows. But we all do.'

'Well, why the hell don't you tell him?' I cried.

'Because he's happy as he is,' said Johnny. 'He's playing the role of the self-sacrificing father. A martyr, if you like. And he loves it. He loves it. Why spoil things by telling him we all know about him?'

'So you're bolstering each other up,' I said. 'Supporting each other on artificial stilts just because you think everything's okay and it's the best way to be.'

Johnny said nothing. Colette pressed her foot against mine. We were, after all, guests in Johnny's car.

Now it all fits into place, I thought. The intense concern Don had shown when Megga had cut his knee, some of the remarks and looks he had given him…yes, it was clear to me now, Don did know.

'Doesn't Don want to tell him?' I said to Johnny.

'No. He thinks the same as us, that Megga's happy as he is, and to leave well alone.'

As we lay in the tent that night, I thought again of the situation. 'Life is too easy for Don now,' I said. 'Perhaps he had it rough before, but now it's too easy. He's destroying himself, and justifying it by thinking he's doing it for Megga's sake.'

'Life?' whispered my wife, seizing on my first word. 'Life? It isn't really life. They've abdicated from life. They're just existing.'

*

For thousands of years, the blue Pacific surf has pounded on the rocks and beaches of Hawaii, and on the following morn its assigned task was to waken my wife and me. The sun at its low angle shone in our eyes. We had breakfast with the boys, then packed our things and made ready to leave. During the night, I had thought deeply about Don and Megga, and had formulated a plan. Now it was time to see if I could make it work.

'I'm going to see Megga when we get into town. Anybody want to come?' I said, looking straight at Don. 'He'll be feeling a bit low. Probably appreciate a visit from one of you.'

Don rose. 'Yeah,' he said. 'I might stroll along with you.'

Good! The first stage of my plan had succeeded.

Johnny spoke. 'I'll give yous a lift. I'm going into town.'

Carl and Fergie immediately smirked. I knew what they were thinking. But Johnny apparently did not notice. We said our goodbyes to Carl and Fergie and Earl, looked around for the last time at the pavilions and surf, and then drove away. I have never seen the park again.

Don sat in the front with Johnny, and Colette and I sat in the back.

I leaned forward. It was time to be bold and honest. 'Going to see your girlfriend, Johnny?' I said.

He showed no reaction. 'Yes.'

'The ice cream girl?'

I could feel Colette's eyes on me, and Don's neck was getting red.

'Yes,' said Johnny, matter-of-factly. 'We're going out for the day.'

'I hope you enjoy it,' I said, and sat back.

My wife dug her fingers into my thigh and looked at me as if to say, you old bastard!

But the real challenge was just beginning. We stopped outside Megga's and said goodbye to Johnny. Don made to walk up the path but I stopped him.

'I'm not going in, Don,' I said.

'What? Why not?'

'Because I know how he is, and I wanted to get you alone.'

'Why?'

'Listen. I know that you're Megga's son. And I know that you know. And I know that Megga doesn't know that you know. And I know all the complicated and silly reasons why you've kept it that way. But listen – no, listen, don't try and put me off. I've seen you, both Colette and I have seen you. You're a sensitive man. You're capable of loving. You've got the potential to be a good citizen, whatever that means. But you've got the ability to live a useful life, useful to yourself and useful to your father! For your sake and for Megga's sake, tell him that you know you're his son.'

'No,' he said. 'You…'

'Listen!' I started to stammer as I sometimes do when I get very intense. 'D-d-do you want t-to live like this f-f-for the rest of your life? M-M-Megga's not going to live for ever, you know!'

'Well now,' he cried in mock triumph, 'there's something wrong with you! You stammer when you're excited! I was beginning to think you were too perfect to be true.'

I gaped. I could feel saliva in my throat.

'Now you listen to me,' he said. 'Who the hell do you think you are, coming into our lives and telling us what's right and what's wrong? D'you think I haven't thought about it?' His eyes seemed to be burning. 'And I'll tell you something else. I'm happy, Megga's happy, everybody's happy. So go back to your smart-arsed university and leave us alone.'

I finally swallowed my saliva. 'Alone, Don? Is that what you want? Alone? Are you really happy? Are you? Then why has Johnny found himself a girlfriend? Why do you all get drunk? No, Don, you're not happy, you're just kidding yourself. Being happy is more than just soaking up the sun and fishing off the rocks and lounging around. Listen, do you know the only times when I've seen you really happy? One was when you examined Colette's foot, another was when you helped Megga with his cut, and the other…'

'I was the only one who knew anything about how to treat them!'

'Exactly, Don! Exactly! You were needed! You were necessary! Don't you see? That was when you were happy: when you were working!'

He was quieter. I knew I was getting through to him.

'When was the other time?' he asked.

'Now, Don,' I said. 'You're happy now! Because you're passionate, you're thinking, you're involved. You're happy now. You can be like that all the time if you give yourself a chance. But it means giving up the park, and that means telling Megga you know you're his son. He loves you, Don. Let him know that you love him!'

I stopped, exhausted. I had pulled out all the stops, given him everything, and now it was up to him. He stared into the distance. From where we stood we could see the distant sea.

I gave it one last effort. 'It would be sink or swim, Don. Like jumping into water. The water of life. And you've got someone to help you swim, instead of both of you sitting on the edge. The bird that sits on the rock all day never takes any risks – and never catches any fish.'

He was still staring at the distant sea. 'Sink or swim, eh,' he said. 'And ol' Johnny's got a girlfriend.' He sighed. 'It's the end of the boys.' Then he said with renewed vigour, 'At least, it's the end of the boys for Johnny and me,' and turning abruptly, he strode up the path to the door of Megga's house.

My wife and I turned away.

'He was right after all,' she said.

'How do you mean?'

'Did you see how he marched up to Megga's door? I believe he is capable of walking six miles in forty minutes.'

'He's capable of anything,' I said.

And standing quietly, we could just hear the distant surf as it pounded, rhythmically, never-ceasing, on the shores of Hawaii, the Big Island, the enchanted island, the island of dreams.

The Great TXM (Grade One) Syndrome

A true story of the future

By the mid twenty-first century, the great Sydney to Melbourne running race had become an established tradition. Its popularity had grown strongly throughout its early years until it was as popular as the Melbourne Cup. Or nearly, anyway.

Probably the most memorable individual performance of all was in 2051, when 'Quiet' Joe Callinan raced up from sixth place with eighty kilometres to go to win in the last kilometre. But the story of what inspired that phenomenal final burst has never been told. Until now.

Joe Callinan had always been a good runner, which was just as well, because he could do bugger-all else. He was known as Quiet Joe because he seldom had anything to say. This was not from a natural reticence but rather because of the fact that Quiet Joe usually didn't know what was going on. To say that he was not over-endowed with intelligence is exaggerating in the extreme. Joe himself often felt that this criticism was rather harsh. Sometimes he *did* know what day it was.

However, after Quiet Joe had won the West Wyalong fun run three years in a row (first prize, a free weekend in Werris Creek, all expenses paid), he decided he was destined for greater things. He got himself a coach, and that is where Young Harry comes in. Why he was called Young Harry is not clear; his surname was Shapiro and he was at least fifteen years older than Quiet Joe, although only about half his size. He had thin weasel-like features and one of those pencil-thin moustaches that is always associated with con men and spivs.

Anyway, to get to that famous day in 2051… By then, a lot of the race was run away from the main highways because of the increasing risk of accidents, and every year the organisers tried to throw in a change of route to keep things fresh. Thus it was that for the first-ever time the race passed through the isolated Rosella Valley some eighty kilometres from the end, and it was there that Quiet Joe collapsed and decided to quit.

He was lying sixth at the time but had no chance of winning, according to everybody, and when sudden hunger and exhaustion hit him in the Rosella Valley he just staggered off the road and into the nearest paddock. Young Harry wasn't with him at the time, having stopped at the village a few kilometres back to buy provisions and chat up the local girls, and when he drove up in his support vehicle, there was Quiet Joe sitting at the side of the road with a bunch of carrot tops in his hand and a look of agony on his face.

'Joe, Joe, what are you doing?' cried Young Harry, jumping down from the van. 'You should be up and running!'

'Jeez, I feel crook,' said Quiet Joe.

'What've you been eating?' said Young Harry. 'Carrots! Where'd you get these?'

Joe pointed behind him. 'Over there. There's rows and rows of 'em.' Then his voice took on a sorry whine. 'I was hungry, Harry. Real hungry, real bad. Harry,' he said with finality, 'I'm quittin'. The carrots've made me crook. I ate too many.' He sank back, exhausted. It was the longest speech he had made in years.

Now one thing you can say in Young Harry's favour, and that is that he knew a crisis when he saw one. His brain moved up a gear as he sank to his knees next to his recumbent charge. He did a thing that few people have ever done, before or since. He applied physical force to Quiet Joe, grabbing him and pulling him to a sitting position. Not many people have applied physical force to Quiet Joe Callinan and got away with it, but right now Joe was a mess. He was virtually in tears.

Young Harry's brain was working overtime. 'Did you say you ate a great bunch of carrots from that paddock?' he cried.

This time, Quiet Joe lived up to his nickname. He just nodded. Miserably.

'Joe, Joe, do you know what you've done!?'

'Yeah, I made meself crook.'

'Joe, Joey me boy, do you know where we are?'

'Course I do,' said Joe. 'We're here.'

'No! I mean yes! 'Course we're here! We're in the Rosella Valley!'

Quiet Joe didn't say anything, but his eyes said, 'So what?'

'The Rosella Valley,' repeated Young Harry. 'This is one of the most famous places in Australia. Not many people know about it but it's very famous. And you know why? 'Cos of the soil, Joe. The best soil in Australia. It's got, er, Tilthoxmolybdenatemagnificat in it. Grade one. Usually called TXM for short. And it's grade one, Joe! There's only about a dozen places in the world that's got TXM grade two. And there's only four places in the whole wide world that's got TXM grade one in its soil! And this is the only one in Australia!'

Quiet Joe's reply was probably the most observant, lucid and intelligent he had ever made in his life. 'Bullshit,' he said.

'It's true,' cried Young Harry. 'I've got a cousin who grows vegetables. He knows about these things. Think of it, Joe.' It was a stupid request to ask Quiet Joe to think of anything, he knew, but Young Harry was in full flight. 'You've eaten a stomach full of carrots containing TXM grade one, when usually a mouthful makes a man feel a king for a week.' His eyes were shining with excitement. 'Joey boy, the stuff from this valley is only made available to the high and mighty. It's too good for the likes of you and me. And you've got a belly full of it!' He spread his hands in an appeal. 'Would I lie to you, Joe? TXM grade one, Joe! And a belly full of it! Joey, you'll be running through the trees instead of round 'em, mate!'

Young Harry looked hard at Quiet Joe. It was the moment of high crisis.

But Joe was looking down the road. 'Jeez, I feel good,' he said.

Young Harry sighed with relief. He opened his mouth to say, 'Up and at 'em, Joe!' but then he saved his breath.

Quiet Joe was already fifty metres down the road and running as if being pursued by the very tax man himself.

Young Harry stood briefly and looked after him. If thoughts such as 'like shooting fish in a barrel' passed through his mind, at least he didn't voice them. He just climbed into his van and sped after his man. Already he was beginning to form a victory speech that he knew he would have to teach Joe word for word.

And that's the true story (they're the only sort I tell) of Quiet Joe Callinan's famous rush up from sixth place with eighty kilometres to go, to catch the leader within a kilometre of the finish and race past him to win by nearly four hundred metres. Of course the press had a field day, calling it the greatest win in the history of the race, which was true, and Young Harry as Quiet Joe's coach managed to cop most of the credit, not to mention his $17\frac{1}{2}$ per cent of Joe's winnings as specified in his contract.

Joe himself kept a low profile. He announced his immediate retirement from running, and headed back to the Rosella Valley with his prize money. He bought himself a nice little forty-hectare farm and now spends his time growing vegetables and trying to convince his potential customers of the fabulous ingredients in his soil. If he is perhaps less successful than he had hoped, at least he is a happy man. He eats nothing but his own produce and he reckons he's getting younger every year.

Young Harry's life took a sadder turn for a long time since that fateful day. He figured he was dead-set to become a politician, but he found the ethics of that profession too dubious even for him. After that, he was a real estate agent, a used car salesman and a pawnbroker, all in quick succession. He couldn't settle down into any of them. But then he hit the jackpot. Right now he's making a fortune as a personal trainer...

The Russian Mafia Cricket Team

Some people have all the luck.

You've probably thought about Arthur Enter, why he should seemingly be endowed with just about every good feature it's possible to have, while others – usually ourselves – hardly seem to have any. Well, for a start, Arthur wasn't always like that. I know, because I come from the same village as he did, and I know his story.

You've no doubt read that he came from our village and eventually went to the big city, where he soon attracted the attention of the national selectors, and that now he's rated as probably the greatest all-rounder we've ever produced. A bowling average first, second or third best ever, depending on how you wangle the statistics; a batting average second only to the immortal Bradman; a faultless slips fielder; and even an excellent wicketkeeper, as he demonstrated that day when he took over from the regular man who broke his nose halfway through the game.

But Arthur wasn't always like that, as I said. Sure, he was a regular member of our village cricket team, but he was only there because he was, in the words of our English captain, 'a damn fine bowler'. He was certainly that. The terror of the other teams. But his batting was, in the words of our Australian vice-captain, 'bloody awful'.

He was the subject of frustration to Bellingham. That's our English captain. Arthur would soon have the other batsmen running for cover – he once took five wickets in five balls, and the next batsman refused to come out – but when it came his turn to bat it was a different story. In eighteen innings, he had scored exactly no runs at all, been out first ball fifteen times, and frankly hadn't looked like scoring. Oh, he knew how to hold a bat all right, he'd seen the others do that, but he had no idea how to wield it and after a while he seemed to give up trying. 'I'm in the team as a bowler,' he'd say.

Then came the day when he retired hurt. It was particularly frustrating to poor old Bellingham, because we only needed three to win, and Arthur only needed to survive one ball to the end of the over.

'Move across,' said Bellingham. 'Cover your wicket. Even if it hits your pad, there's the chance you'll be given not out.'

So Arthur moved across. But the ball didn't hit his pad. It hit his – well, what the commentators carefully call 'the groin'.

Poor Arthur was carried off the field in agony and we had to relinquish the match. We left him in the hands of our physiotherapist and drove away in disgust to drown our sorrows at the pub.

It may seem strange to you that a village team should have an official physiotherapist, but Julia Thigh worked in a clinic in the city during the week and donated her time to the team for a few hours at the weekend.

She was a nice girl, and interesting. For a start, Julia Thigh wasn't the name she was born with. She was born Julia Smith, but when she came to our village at the age of eighteen, the locals figured that was far too dull a name for her, and got to calling her Julia Thigh, on account of she often wore short skirts. Far from resenting this, Julia embraced the nickname and soon started calling herself Julia Thigh, and eventually changed it to that by deed poll.

By the time she was twenty-two, Julia was seriously looking for a husband. She was a methodical girl and would tally up the advantages and disadvantages of each of the eligible bachelors in the neighbourhood. She wasn't getting very far until she came across Arthur.

Arthur had some very good points. He had the body of a god, the looks of a film star; he didn't smoke, never got drunk, was gentle and courteous except when bowling; and his parents owned a farm, which meant that one day he would be rich. All of them very fine advantages.

And there was only one disadvantage. He was as thick as a brick.

Anyway, as I said, we left her to look after him and went to the pub. Arthur eventually joined us and seemed dreamily happy, even when Bellingham chastised him yet again for his hopeless batting.

The next week was a grudge match against the neighbouring village.

Halfway through our batting session, Arthur went to Julia and said,

'I'm not quite properly recovered from my injury of last week. Could you give me a bit more treatment please?' He looked just like a sheep pleading for its life.

Julia was equal to this particular challenge. 'Only if you score ten runs,' she said.

Well! I've played a lot of cricket and watched a lot more, but I can honestly say that I've never seen such concentration in a batsman as I saw in Arthur that day. I know because I was the batsman at the other end. We were the last pair in. And when Arthur had somehow scraped two runs together, he called to me, 'Don't you get out now and leave me stranded!'

I nearly fell over in surprise. But I didn't get out, and when Arthur was on six he clipped a neat shot through mid-wicket for four to bring up his ten runs. He jumped and punched the air as though he'd scored a hundred, and jubilation was written all over his face.

He was out the next ball.

But he didn't care. He disappeared for his treatment for a few minutes and came back just in time for us to take the field. His bowling seemed a bit subdued for a while but he eventually revved up and we beat our arch-enemies for the first time in four years.

That was the start of a revolution. The next week, Julia wanted fifteen runs out of him – and got them. Then it was twenty; then thirty; and pretty soon Arthur was practising batting for hours on end just like the great Bradman himself.

It was obvious that he was in love. Whatever Julia asked of him, he would provide. She knew he hadn't enough brains to hang his hat on, but his other attributes surely outweighed them.

And when, at the start of the next season, Arthur announced that he'd been asked to play for the top team in the big city, Julia accompanied him as his personal physio. That was only natural, because by that time she was also his wife.

They made an unstoppable couple. Arthur went from strength to strength. It wasn't long before he was playing for the state team, and there was talk that the national selectors were watching him.

We all hoped he'd get into the national team and give them a boost, because they were going through a bad patch at the time and needed an infusion of energy. But Arthur wouldn't be able to do all that himself.

I knew what was needed, of course. But how to make it happen – that was the problem.

Then we had a stroke of luck. Arthur occasionally came back to play with us when he was free from his other duties. And of course Julia came with him.

It is necessary here to acquaint you more closely with our Australian vice-captain. His name was Charlie Tarr. We called him Bitumen for short. He was a decent bloke, pretty good at most sports and, like a typical Aussie, was more interested in sport than his job. But he had been hopeless with women. After all the local girls had rejected him, he finally married one of those Russian women who advertise in the newspapers.

Olga was a fine, imposing figure of a woman. Not unattractive in an Eastern European sort of way, totally uninterested in cricket and – well, let's just say that she didn't stand for any nonsense. It was rumoured that she had connections to the Russian mafia, but I don't know about that. All I know is that Bitumen seemed happy with her and made sure he never upset her.

Anyway, on this particular day, Arthur came back to play with us. And this time – oh, providence be praised! – it was Bitumen who suffered the indignity of being hit in the unmentionables. He wasn't wearing a protective box, mainly because he discovered too late that someone had nicked it from his bag and he didn't have time to search for it before he went out to bat.

He stumbled back to the sideline and collapsed into the waiting arms of Julia, who took him to the massage room to fix him up.

Oh, she fixed him up all right! I got it all on camera, just after I put his protective box back in his bag.

My plan was working perfectly.

Despite Bitumen's injury, we won the game and retired to the pub to celebrate. After a few drinks, when everyone had relaxed and half the boys had gone home, I took Julia Thigh to one side and explained the situation to her. I emphasised the hints about Olga Tarr's alleged connections to the Russian mafia, and made it clear what a formidable enemy she would be if she ever found out about Julia's cure for Bitumen.

Julia went pale and I knew she understood. 'Okay,' she said. 'What do you want?'

Now, I'm a good man. I could have got really sleazy at this point. But my nobler instincts came to the fore. 'I want you to become the physiotherapist for the whole national cricket team.'

She gasped. 'How am I going to do that?'

I didn't answer. I just held up the negatives of the photos and reminded her once again of Olga's (alleged) connections to the Russian mafia.

Well, it took some time, of course. It wasn't long before Arthur was playing for the national team with Julia as his personal physio; and I figure she used his success to wheedle her way into that position for the whole team.

That's when we took off. The national team, I mean. It's not that they had an infusion of new blood or anything like that. They just seemed to be more motivated, concentrated harder and showed obvious joy when they achieved their goals.

Arthur quickly became the star of the team. He was never the captain – he was too thick for that – but as I said at the start, his batting and bowling averages were of the highest order.

And Julia became established as the team's physiotherapist. For the first time in years, there was intense competition to get into the team. And that of course raised the standard.

I often used to ponder on the irony that, if motivation can be traced like a family tree, the common ancestor of our national team's striving to do well was probably a small group of Russian toughs somewhere in the wilds of Eastern Europe, who knew nothing about cricket and cared even less.

All of that was some twenty years ago. Arthur has retired now and so has Julia. But their legacy lives on. They had two children. The oldest is a boy who, frankly, has been something of a disappointment to them. He came top of his class in poetry and he plays chess, for goodness' sake.

Their daughter Virginia, however, is a girl to be proud of. She's a nice girl, and interesting. When she left high school last year, she went to college to study to be a physiotherapist, like her mother. She had to do some practical work on massage for her course, and she chose our cricket team to practise on.

We've just had our most successful season in years.

The Story of Melting Snows

Taken from an old Eskimo legend

But it was warm inside as she snuggled up to her husband. Inishtook – the name meant 'Righteous Man' – was a good provider whose sharp eye and sharper reflexes guaranteed her food and warmth throughout the year. And that was enough to make her a very lucky woman in the tribe. Good hunters were rare and therefore precious. The women merely bore babies, extra mouths to feed, if they survived, until they were old enough to hunt for themselves.

Eginwah – 'Melting Snows' – was lucky to have such a good hunter for a husband. But the price demanded by the wild Arctic wastes often brought tears and always brought heartache. Inishtook was her second husband. It was not unusual for a woman to have four or even five husbands during a lifetime. The Arctic always craved its share of slaughter.

A hunter might last six, seven years before the cruel white death came to claim him. A good hunter might last twelve, fourteen years. An excellent hunter, twenty. But it always ended the same way: an ice floe, a crevasse, an unexpected blizzard, snow-blindness, frostbite too far gone, a shooting accident. Or maybe nothing more than sheer exhaustion. Something, always something to claim them. Good hunters were rare. Inishtook was a good hunter.

But now the price was being asked again. Inishtook must go and hunt for food. The seals were good and he must take them while they were plentiful. Tonight was his last night. Melting Snows would not see him again for eight or ten days. In the warm shack, under the bearskin rugs in the dim light of the tallow candle, she lay close with him. Her warmth would help him in the cruel cold days ahead. But when her husband slept at last, she lay for a long time with her eyes open.

Inishtook rose very early in the morning and started to prepare the dogs for the journey. Melting Snows prepared his food. Seegloo, her brother, called to them cheerfully from his neighbouring shack and walked across to give Inishtook the traditional wish of a plentiful bounty. The creases came to the corner of Inishtook's eyes as he accepted his brother-in-law's good wishes. The two men liked each other. Often they went hunting together.

When Inishtook was gone, Melting Snows sat and talked to Seegloo and his wife Kotah for a while, but soon returned to her own shack to commence her day's work. She had meat to prepare, skins to cure and tallow candles to make. When she was gone, Seegloo and Kotah talked about her in low tones, occasionally glancing in the direction of her hut. Melting Snows did her chores automatically, thinking of other things.

*

The wind whistled icily across the frozen lake and Ooqueah knew that it was time to return to the village. The wind was from the north and Ooqueah – the name meant 'Lucky Hunter' – knew that it would last for at least five days. The lake would be frozen too thick to break for fish, the bears were all gone and this was not seal country. It was time to return with his bounty. He looked forward to being at the village for a while. He enjoyed the companionship of his neighbours and he loved to joke with his friends. With any luck, he would see his woman and spend some time with her. Ooqueah was one of the best hunters in the village. He was young, vigorous and he loved life. Truly was he a lucky hunter.

He packed his gear, paying meticulous attention to the way it was bound to the sled. It was piled high when at last he roused the dogs and harnessed them. The wind was coming with a constantly low, mournful sound and Ooqueah knew that a storm was on the way. If the dogs pulled well and he was lucky, he would get to the village in time. The thought of the village cheered and invigorated him and he yelled his dogs into action. They strained. He pushed. The load was big and heavy. Despite the cold, his armpits and his groin were sweaty, and the dogs' tongues were lolling, before the sled moved; and then they were off.

Once they were moving, it was good. The snow was hard under the runners and the dogs got into the heavy rhythm of pulling. Ooqueah thought about the village, and about his woman. He thought of her warmth. He thought of the welcome of her bed. He thought of her arms, her legs wrapped round him. He thought of how his hard hunter's body would succumb to her so that in the end she would be triumphant. Then he thought of what the other people would be thinking as he lay in his woman's bed. And despite the effort of pushing the sled, suddenly he felt a shiver. For a few brief seconds, his pushing lacked its customary enthusiasm.

*

The short Arctic night was descending when Inishtook stopped his dogs and made a hurried camp. He had been hurrying all day. He had covered much ground and he wanted to rise early to continue. At this time of year, the night only allowed him four or five hours of darkness. As soon as he had cared for the dogs and made his camp, he ate and then went straight to bed. It was not long before he slept, and his last thoughts of the day were of his wife.

*

At about the same time as Inishtook was making camp, Ooqueah arrived in the village. The barking of the village dogs heralded his arrival, and soon he was surrounded by happy Eskimo faces eager to observe his bounty and listen to his ready tongue. Ooqueah worked hard unpacking his sled as he talked and laughed with his neighbours. But as darkness fell and he finished unpacking, they drifted away until he was left alone. He

95

knew there were some people in the village who had not come to greet
him, and he knew why. He fed his dogs, then went inside his shack and
washed. When he was finished, he stood and listened for a time. The wind
was howling: the storm had come. The people were making the most of
the short night. He opened his shack door and stepped out. The cold
made him hunch up instinctively as he crossed to his woman's hut and
quickly entered. His woman looked up and then relaxed when she saw
who it was. She had been expecting him.

*

An Arctic storm is an awesome thing. It starts quietly, almost gently.
Black clouds form on the horizon as though gathering together for a mass
attack. Then the temperature drops: drops to thirty degrees below zero
so that the breath forms a frost on the chin, so that it is painful merely
to breathe, so that to drive against it means that the eyeballs will freeze.
The wind whistles low and mournfully, and then the black clouds start to
advance. Slowly they come at first, but then they speed up as though they
see their goal. And then the first snow comes.

A few flakes blown by the wind, tumbling past; and then the gloom is
here as the clouds come overhead, and the snow starts to come in profusion.
The wind has risen to a howl, a long, fearful portent of death. It is dark,
the clouds are everywhere, and the snow is driving, cutting, lashing as it
goes before the wind, the wind that batters, screams, shouts and rages with
its icy breath, and the snow is a prison of death in the darkness, a raging,
tumbling, agonising vault of frozen death. Then when it seems the peak
has been reached, the blackness intensifies, the cold cuts deeper, the wind
screams louder and the driving, driving, driving snow buries everything in
its overwhelming force. The very soul of the earth gasps for survival, clinging,
holding on somehow to life as this battering ram of nature rides over it.

And then it is gone. The clouds are scudding away, the wind is dying,
the snow is descending gently and the cold has lost its knife edge. It is
light. A breeze blows. It is clear. The storm has gone.

But while it lasted, no man could have survived unprotected in it. While it lasted, he would have had to succumb so that in the end it would have been triumphant.

*

But it was warm inside as she lay next to her lover. Her eyes were wide open and she thought clearly while he snored by her side.

Inishtook, she thought, is a good hunter, one of the best in the tribe. And so is this man, also one of the tribe's best. But Inishtook has the first thoughts of suspicion in him. This storm, although it is over, may make him change his plans and return. But it really makes little difference. Too many of my neighbours know about it for it to be kept from him much longer. The two men are bound to have a showdown sooner or later. And that means only one thing: death for one, possible crippling for the other. And it will all have been because of me. I will be to blame. I am to blame. I am a woman, I bear hungry, demanding children. I am causing dissension in the tribe. The tribe must be happy. We must be united to survive. The two men are quarrelling over me and I will be the only one to blame for the death of a good man. Without me, they have no cause to fight. Without me…

The thought gnawed at her. It would not let her go, it caused her brain actual physical pain as it gnawed and gnawed into her consciousness. But there was no other way. It must be done. It was a simple choice.

Slowly, slowly, carefully she eased out of bed. She knew what she was looking for and where to find it. Her lover snored on. Slowly she opened the door and stepped out, carrying the small hard object that would serve her purpose. Her last thought was, 'Now the tribe will have no more problems because of me.'

*

Because of the permafrost, burial of corpses is impractical in the Arctic. The Eskimo practice is to clean and wash the dead body, and dress the women's hair. The body is then wrapped in a blanket or animal skin and laid out in the tundra face up and covered with stones.

Inishtook, the Righteous Man, arranged the ritual. The tribe gathered together at a respectful distance and stood silently until it was time to leave.

At a distance from the tribe stood Ooqueah, the Lucky Hunter, also silent and respectful. When the short ceremony was over, the tribe walked back to the village. But Ooqueah had packed his sled and now he moved in the opposite direction. The desolate Arctic waste spread out before him. He knew that from now on he might not be such a lucky hunter.

Well I'll Be Damned

I was glad when Mr Whitehouse finally discovered I'd been borrowing his books on Africa. I was beginning to think he'd never find out. The other servants watched with wide eyes as Mrs Whitehouse, thin and ascetic – the old bitch! – triumphantly marched me up the stairs and into his office. She closed the door slowly as she went out, and I reckoned she'd be listening at the keyhole. I couldn't do anything about that.

I stood in front of Mr Whitehouse's desk. It was now or never. You've got to be a good judge of character in my profession, and this was good training, I thought, to weigh him up and see if I was right.

He coughed hesitantly and I knew I had a good start. 'Now, Doris,' he said, 'what's all this about Mrs Whitehouse finding my book on early missionaries in Angola in your room? There seems to be no doubt you stole it, but what I can't understand is, why? Why would you want to take some dry-as-dust thing like that, eh? Mm?'

'Oh, Mr Whitehouse,' I pleaded (you've got to be a good actor in my business, and this was good training again), 'they're not dry-as-dust at all. They're very interesting. I'm sorry I borrowed your books but I haven't damaged any of them.'

'Now wait a minute, wait a minute,' he said. (He's perplexed. It's going wonderfully.) 'Do you mean to say you've borrowed other books before you stole this one?'

'Oh no, Mr Whitehouse. I mean yes. I mean…' (Good! He could see I was getting confused.) 'I mean, I was not stealing *Early Missionaries in Angola*, I'm only borrowing it, sir. I've borrowed some others too, but I always returned them and they're completely undamaged. *Rhodesia in the Nineteenth Century* had ten pages missing when I borrowed it, sir.'

'You mean to tell me you're taking my books, reading them, and then returning them without my knowledge?'

'Not all of your books, sir. Only…' (A subtle little hesitation here.) '…only the ones on Africa, sir.'

'And why are you so interested in Africa, may I ask?' His tone had just that edge of vexation in it.

It was time to be contrite. 'Well, sir, I'm sorry I borrowed your books, sir, but – well, I want to go to Africa, sir. And I want to learn all I can about it before I go, sir. That's the only reason I borrowed your books, sir, and I haven't damaged any of them, sir.'

Most men are at a loss when a woman cries. When they see she is about to start, they feel cornered.

'But didn't it occur to you, Doris, that you could have asked me to lend you the books?'

'Oh, I was afraid you might refuse, sir, and then I would have had no chance to read them at all.'

Almost in tears. Ask me! Ask me now!

'Oh, come now, Doris, you know that I would have lent you the books if you really wanted to read them.'

Ask me! Ask me!

'But why in heaven's name do you want to go to Africa, Doris?'

Ah!

'Well, sir…' (A hesitant biting of the lower lip, then a gathering of courage, a full look in the face.) 'I want to be a missionary, sir. I'm going as soon as I've saved enough money, and…'

'A missionary, Doris? In Africa?'

'Yes, sir. Oh, please sir, don't sack me, sir! I'm saving as hard as I can to go but if I'm out of work I'll never make it, sir. I promise I won't touch your books again, sir. I promise.'

'Well, I'll be damned,' he said. (He hasn't been listening. Good.) 'A missionary in Africa, eh, Doris?'

'Yes, sir,' I said in a still, small voice.

'Well, I'll be damned,' he said again. He seemed to think for a few moments, then a frown came on his face. Difficulties ahead. He leaned forward. 'Doris, do you have any idea what it's like in Africa?' he said. 'It may be a land of exotic birds and butterflies and all that sort of thing, but I tell you now it's also a land of snakes and spiders, and of poverty and bitter degradation. It's a terribly savage place. You wouldn't last five minutes.'

'Oh, sir, please don't try and discourage me, sir,' I said. 'I'm not a religious fanatic, but I know I can help them.'

'Let me tell you something, Doris. This may come as a surprise to you, but I worked as a missionary once, for two years. Not in Africa, but in China. And it's hard work, Doris. It's very hard and frustrating work. I lasted two years and then I came back.'

I was genuinely very surprised. I knew he was a regular churchgoer, but I had always thought that that was just part of being the Respected Country Gentleman.

'Yes, Doris,' he continued. 'I was glad to get back. Then when the Kaiser started the Great War, I was glad to go as an officer, just so that I wouldn't be called back to China again. That's how hard I found it!'

At that moment, I was almost sorry for what I was doing. He had earned new respect from me. But I had set my course. There was no going back now.

'But you don't even know anything about the African languages, do you, Doris?'

I shook my head, almost in tears again. This was the real crisis point. There was a long pause.

Then he said again, 'Well, I'll be damned.'

I literally held my breath.

'Tell you what I'll do, Doris,' he said suddenly. (Here it comes, here it comes!)

'There's a friend of mine, Colonel Farndon, who spent a lot of time in Africa and who knows Swahili quite well. That's one of the major languages, Doris. I'm sure he would be willing to teach you. In your own time, of course. And I'll tell you what: if you can satisfy the colonel in three months that you've learnt the language well enough, I'll pay your fare to Cape Town.' He sat back, proud of himself. 'How's that?'

Well, that was near enough to a knockout win for me. My judgement of him had been right. And I'm not completely unintelligent. I could learn Swahili good enough.

The bitch Mrs Whitehouse was sourer than ever. I reckon she bawled him out for it, but he was a good old stick and wouldn't take it to heart. She gave me the dirtiest jobs from then on, and always tried to conceive something that would make me miss my appointment with the colonel, but the old man seemed to be around at the right moment every time and made sure I got away.

Colonel Farndon, with his iron-grey hair and strong face, gave the impression of a man still vigorous at sixty. He told me that Swahili was an easy language to learn, but I found it hard enough. Sometimes I wondered if it was worth it, but I stuck at it. The fare to Cape Town was a lot of money.

Three months – three hard months – passed. I wondered if I was going to be good enough to satisfy the colonel.

One night, at the end of the lesson, he said to me, 'It's time you showed me what you know, Doris. Come prepared for something of a test next time, will you.'

I figured it would be a written test, and I planned accordingly. A few written phrases on the inside of my thigh, where only I could see when I sat down and pulled my skirt up a little, and I was ready.

It worked beautifully. The colonel had prepared a paper, and sat and read a book while I did the exam.

He read through my answers and seemed puzzled. 'Doris,' he said at length, 'your paper is very inconsistent. There are some parts where you're not very good at all, I'm afraid. Yet there are others where you are one hundred per cent correct. It almost makes me think you might have been cheating.'

What did he know?

'That would not be very good, Doris my dear,' he continued, 'because then I would have to tell Mister Whitehouse that you had not...er... satisfied me...'

Ah! So it was judgement of character time again, was it?

I lowered my eyes guiltily and allowed myself a slight blush. 'I'm afraid so,' I said breathlessly.

He seemed a little breathless himself.

'I'll show you where I wrote a few phrases.' I pulled my skirt up and showed him the Swahili words on my inner thigh: a very nice inner thigh, even if I say it myself. And the colonel seemed to agree…

'She satisfied me completely,' said the colonel to Mr Whitehouse the next day. 'She's very good.'

'Thank you, colonel,' I said. 'I enjoyed it.'

'Well,' said Mr Whitehouse, 'I'm a man of my word. When would you like to go, Doris?'

'I would like to go as soon as I can, sir.'

'No time like the present,' he said cheerily, and picked up the telephone.

*

They came down to the railway station to say goodbye: servants and all. There were the usual sad faces, wishes of good luck, and I even managed to squeeze a tear out.

'You've been so good to me,' I said. 'All of you.' I even included (officially) Mrs Whitehouse in that.

After we had waved goodbye, I sat back in the train for a few minutes until it reached the next station. Then I got out and went to the phone.

They told me they would have to keep ten per cent because of the late cancellation. I couldn't do anything about that. Ninety per cent of the fare to Cape Town is still a lot of money. Then I took my suitcase and booked into a cheap room until the money came through.

I had it all figured out. The house, the girls, and the sort of clientele we'd be aiming at. I even got Robin Maskell to work as our bouncer. He's a homosexual. It's safer that way. But he's big and strong and he knows how to handle an unruly customer. Officially, he's the maintenance man.

As I said, in my profession you've got to have your head screwed on.

We prospered. The police were easy enough to manage, Robin was the ideal strong-arm man and, even though I say it myself, I am a good organiser. I even had two special girls which is the mark of a high-class organisation: a 'go away' girl and a 'come back for more' girl. Valerie was our go-away girl. If I didn't like a man or didn't want him to come back, I'd give him Valerie. Her natural disposition, which of course I encouraged, was to repulse him and make him wish he'd never wasted his money in such a crummy joint. Georgina, on the other hand, was trained to make the men think they'd walked straight into paradise. She was a beauty. I used her for the good payers and for the men we liked to have around, who would protect us by their influence if trouble ever came.

As I said, we prospered. And we still are doing, although I don't know for how much longer.

You see, last night my assistant Maria and I were sitting in the room where we can see the men as they come in but they can't see us, when suddenly I said, 'Well, I'll be damned.'

Maria was surprised. 'I've never heard you say that before,' she said.

I smiled inwardly as I remembered that traumatic interview of nearly six years ago – because who had come in but Mr Whitehouse himself! It gave me quite a shock, I can tell you. I never thought he was that sort, although when I think of that thin ascetic bitch of his wife, perhaps I could understand it. I don't know what he would have done if he'd seen me. I don't know which of us would have been the most embarrassed.

Anyway, it threw me into a dilemma. The dangers of his coming here were obvious, and yet – he was the man who had helped me start out in business. Should I repulse him, or should I thank him? Valerie or Georgina, that was the question.

I turned to Maria. 'The tall gentleman who just came in,' I said, 'the distinguished-looking man with the white moustache.'

She nodded.

'I want you to go to him and tell him he's our millionth customer, or something like that, and he can have this one free. Give him Georgina and tell him he can take as long as he likes. Then write him a card to say he can come back for free as many times as he likes in the next twelve months, provided he lets us know first when he's coming. Oh, and one other thing: if you mention my name to him at all, ever, I'll see that you never work in this city again. You got all that?'

'I sure have,' she said. 'But gee! Is he your father or something?'

'No, he's not my father,' I said. 'But I know him. He was instrumental in my learning Swahili.'

'I never knew you could speak Swahili.'

'Haven't you got things to do?' I said.

She gave me a queer look as she went out, but I didn't mind.

But now I'm worried. They say that once you start getting a soft heart in my profession, you're doomed.

Motor neurone disease (MND) is the name given to a group of diseases in which the nerve cells (neurones) controlling the muscles that enable us to move, speak, breathe and swallow undergo degeneration and die. Motor function is controlled by the upper motor neurones in the brain that descend to the spinal cord; these neurones activate lower motor neurones. The lower motor neurones exit the spinal cord and directly activate muscles. With no nerves to activate them, muscles gradually weaken and waste. MND can affect a person's ability to walk, speak, swallow and breathe. Each day in Australia two people die from MND. There is no known cure and no effective treatment.

The Motor Neurone Disease Association of Tasmania assists people living with MND and their carers by providing useful and informative information, assisting with equipment needs, raising the profile of the disease in the community and raising funds for research.

www.ingramcontent.com/pod-product-compliance
Lightning Source LLC
Chambersburg PA
CBHW030214130726
47898CB00012B/1016